GLADIATOR SCHOOL

BOOK 4

BLOOD VENGEANCE

DAN SCOTT

SCRIBO

A division of Book House

First published in Great Britain by Scribo MMXIV
Scribo, a division of Book House, an imprint of
The Salariya Book Company
25 Marlborough Place, Brighton, BN1 1UB
www.salariya.com

ISBN 978-1-909645-62-2

The right of Dan Scott to be identified as the author of this work has been asserted
in accordance with sections 77 and 78 of the Copyright, Designs
and Patents Act, 1988.

Book Design by David Salariya

Printed and bound in India

The text for this book is set in Cochin
The display type is P22 Durer Caps

www.scribobooks.com

GLADIATOR SCHOOL

BOOK 4

BLOOD VENGEANCE

DAN SCOTT

SCRIBO

A division of Book House

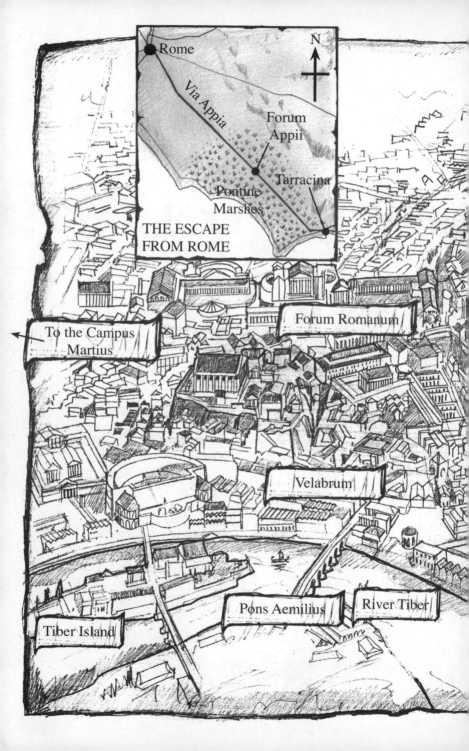

N

Rome

Via Appia

Forum Appii

Tarracina

Pontine Marshes

THE ESCAPE FROM ROME

Forum Romanum

To the Campus Martius

Velabrum

Pons Aemilius

River Tiber

Tiber Island

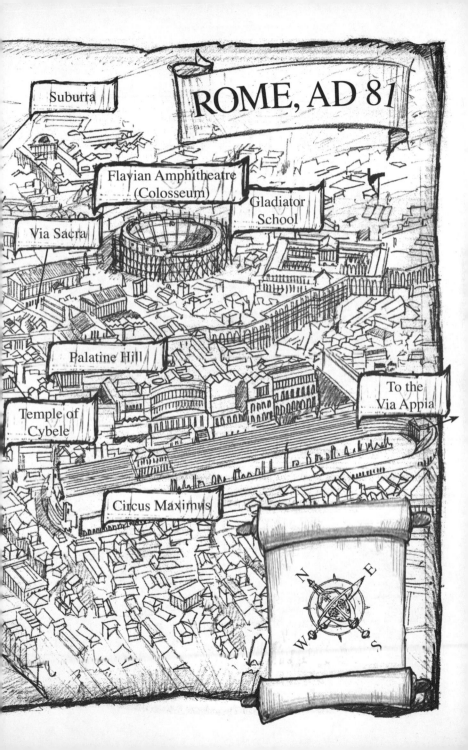

LUCIUS'S TRAVELS IN THE MEDITERRANEAN

Rome

Tarracina

Tyrrhenian Sea

Mediterranean Sea
(Mare Nostrum)

Carthage

Africa

KEY

→ Voyage of the slave ship

⇢ Voyage of the *Concordia*

⋯▸ Voyage of the *Cygnus*

Introducing Gladiator School, a series of novels set in a rich and textured world of dusty arenas, heated battles, fierce loyalty and fiercer rivalry. Follow young Lucius as his privileged life is suddenly turned upside down, leading him to seek answers amongst the slaves and warriors who work and train at Rome's gladiator school.

Reader reviews of Gladiator School 2: *Blood & Fire*

'There are fights in dusty arenas, traitors, disappearances, family loyalty, criminals and gladiatorial games. All very exciting and a great adventurous read for kids that like a bit of action and a bit of history in their novels. My son said these books were really exciting.'
BECKY GODDARD-HILL, BOOK REVIEWS FOR MUMS

'Pompeii itself is accurately described . . . as a rough-and-tumble almost "frontier" town . . . Scott has also obviously carefully researched the stages of the Vesuvian eruption and expertly worked them into the plot line. Once more suspense propels the narrative and narrow escapes should keep young readers turning the pages eagerly.'
MARY HARRSCH, ROMAN TIMES

'The story continues with all the attention to compelling detail that won it so many fans. Action adventure, Romans, gladiators and so much more, brought to life for readers of 9+ in a series that captivates readers both young and old.'
GERRY MAYFIELD, OUR BOOK REVIEWS ONLINE

What the lovereading4kids reader reviewers said about Gladiator School 1: *Blood Oath*

'I would not put it down.'
GRACE PARKER, AGE 10

'It's brilliant; it has a mix of different genres so it is suitable for everyone. You will love it!!!'
CHRISTOPHER TANNER, AGE 11

'It made me feel like I was actually in Ancient Rome with Lucius.'
LUCY MINTON, AGE 9

'There is only one single bad thing about this book and that is that it ends!'
ADAM GRAHAM, AGE 9

'I . . . liked the way it told you what the Roman word meant in English – it was really interesting.'
CARLA McGUIGAN, AGE 12

'If you like adventures with a touch of mystery you will love this book.'
SAM HARPER, AGE 9

'I was sitting on the edge of my seat wondering what was going to happen next.'
SHAKRIST MASUPHAN-BOODLE, AGE 10

THE MAIN CHARACTERS

Lucius, a Roman boy

Quintus, his older brother

Valeria, their young sister

Aquila, their father

Caecilia, their mother

Isidora, Lucius's friend, a freedwoman
(ex-slave) from Egypt

Gracchus, a lanista (trainer of gladiators)
at Carthage

Hierax, a travelling lanista

Crassus, a lanista at Rome

Eprius, a young patrician (nobleman)
from Pompeii

ROME
AD 81

THE STORY SO FAR...

Until the age of thirteen, Lucius Valerius Aquila had led a happy, comfortable life as the middle child of a well-to-do Roman family. His father, Quintus Valerius Aquila, was a respected senator, and they lived in a luxurious house in Rome.

All that changed one day in early July, AD 79. That was the day Lucius's father disappeared, just in time to avoid being arrested for treason. Aquila was accused of being the Spectre – the ruthless informer whose reports had sent many people to their deaths under the previous emperor, Vespasian. Now the new emperor, Titus, was determined to end the practice of informing. Lucius was sure his father was innocent. Yet everyone else, his family included, seemed to accept that Aquila must be the Spectre.

And with Aquila gone, Lucius and his family had to face the sudden loss of their home, wealth and status. Lucius's uncle, Gaius Valerius Ravilla, became their protector. He sold off their beautiful house, their slaves and most of their possessions, and installed Lucius, along with his mother Caecilia and his younger sister Valeria, in a cramped flat in an unfashionable part of Rome called Suburra.

Meanwhile, Lucius's older brother, Quintus Valerius Felix (known to his family as Quin), shocked everyone by giving up his citizen status and enrolling as a gladiator. Quin persuaded Ravilla to give him a try-out at his gladiator school, the Ludus Romanus. Anxious for his brother's safety, Lucius got himself a job at the school, so he could keep an eye on Quin while working for the school's tough lanista (trainer), Crassus. The work was strenuous and dull, his only consolation being a budding friendship with one of his co-workers, an Egyptian slave girl called Isidora.

One day, to his great joy, Lucius received news of his father. Rufus, a new fighter at the school, revealed himself as Aquila's personal slave. He told Lucius that Aquila knew where proof of his innocence could be found, and he needed Lucius to help him get hold of it. Aquila wanted to explain everything in person, but before Rufus could lead Lucius to his father, Ravilla had Rufus put to death. It was now clear that Ravilla was not the kindly uncle Lucius had taken him for. In fact, Ravilla hated his brother Aquila and would do anything to ensure he remained in exile. Lucius was now convinced that Ravilla had been behind the accusations that had forced Aquila to flee.

These suspicions were confirmed a few weeks later when Lucius and Quin were selected to be part of a troupe from the Ludus Romanus being sent to the city of Pompeii to compete in a festival of games. While in Pompeii, Lucius learned the shocking truth that Ravilla was, in fact, the Spectre. This made Ravilla's denouncement of Aquila even more monstrous. He must have accused Aquila of being the Spectre both to destroy him and, at the same time, to cover up his own guilt. The visit to Pompeii may have revealed the truth about Ravilla's duplicity, but in another way it turned out to be spectacularly mis-timed: Lucius and Quin barely escaped with their lives when the nearby mountain, Vesuvius, erupted, engulfing the city in a fiery surge.

Six months after his return from Pompeii, Lucius was working as an animal handler with his friend Isidora, preparing wild beasts for their appearance in the Inaugural Games of the newly built Flavian Amphitheatre. One day, Lucius bumped into his former tutor Agathon, who showed him a message he had recently received from Lucius's father. Aquila explained that proof of his innocence existed in the form of a letter from the previous emperor, Vespasian, confirming that Ravilla, not Aquila, was the Spectre.

Aquila believed that his brother had this letter in his possession, and he wanted Lucius to try and retrieve it for him.

Lucius, Agathon, Isidora and Valeria plotted to steal the letter and, after numerous setbacks, they finally managed to get hold of it. Meanwhile, Quin was finding fame and glory in the arena, first as a gladiator, and later as a bestiarius, or beast-fighter. Quin had always been convinced of his father's guilt, and it was a great shock for him to see the letter and realise how wrong he had been.

Unfortunately, before they could show the letter to anyone, it was destroyed in a fire deliberately started by Ravilla's agents. The fire also killed Agathon, leaving Lucius close to despair. Quin, however, remained optimistic. He was sure he could use his fame to denounce Ravilla and restore his father's reputation – with or without the letter. But before he could do so, he was charged with the arson attack and flung into prison. Ravilla, determined to silence Quin before he could speak out, had hired some 'eyewitnesses' to say they had seen Quin light the fire.

As punishment, Quin was forced to face wild animals alone in the arena, unarmed and without protection. He was about to be killed by a tiger when Isidora made a dramatic entrance and the ferocious cat instantly became as gentle as a kitten. Unbeknownst to the awestruck spectators, girl and tiger had previously become close after she had nursed it back to health. Emperor Titus interpreted Isidora's intervention as a message from the gods, and Quin was spared.

When the emperor visited Quin in hospital, Lucius took the opportunity to urge Titus to look again at the case of his father. Lucius spoke of the letter from Vespasian that had been burned. A courtier then pointed out that there were copies in the palace archive of every letter Vespasian had ever sent.

A copy of the letter was duly found: documentary proof of Aquila's innocence and Ravilla's treachery. Aquila was immediately recalled from exile and had his property and status fully restored. He was reunited with his family amid scenes of great rejoicing. Meanwhile, Ravilla, facing dishonour and death, opted to take his own life.

Lucius tried to persuade the newly freed Isidora to come and live with his family in their house on the Esquiline Hill in Rome, but she wished to make her home in Egypt, the land of her parents' birth. Lucius returned to his scholarly studies, while Quin, by now disillusioned with the gladiatorial life, resolved to forge a new career as a chariot racer in the Circus Maximus…

CHARIOTS
OF FIRE

ROME
12 SEPTEMBER AD 81

It was the eighth day of the Ludi Romani – the Roman Games. Marcus Acilius Glabrio, Consul of Rome* and sponsor of the games, dropped his white cloth, signalling the start of the race. The twelve starting gates sprang open and out charged the charioteers. The air exploded with the exhilarated cries of 150,000 spectators, as hoofbeats echoed like thunder around the vast, elongated bowl of the Circus Maximus.

Lucius, seated in the stands next to his father, Aquila, strained to identify his brother Quintus among the racers, but all he could see at first was horses and

---

* *Consul of Rome: one of a pair of high-ranking officials appointed by the emperor.*

clouds of dust. The bright sunlight forced him to squint. Then the charioteers came into view, biceps gleaming as they gripped the reins and lashed their horses, urging them faster. The drivers, hunched in their flimsy wooden chariots, were dressed in simple tunics in their team colours – red, white, blue and green. Each team was running three chariots today, and each chariot was pulled by a team of four horses, making for a crowded track. Lucius, who had never previously been the slightest bit interested in chariot racing, was now a firm fan of the Whites, but only because it was Quin's team.

'There he is!' he cried, suddenly spotting Quin's dusty white tunic and golden-blond curls poking out from beneath his helmet. 'He's second, I think – or maybe third.' There were so many chariots all bunched together, it was hard to be sure.

Lucius and Aquila were in the senatorial seats to the right of the imperial box, on the opposite side of the stadium to the starting gates. They momentarily lost sight of the chariots as they passed behind a towering red granite obelisk, located halfway along the spina – the strip that ran down the centre of the long, oval track. When Quin appeared again, his chariot was hemmed in among a cluster of others, close to the high stone wall of the spina.

'Why are they crowding him like that?' Lucius shouted, alarmed.

'I have no idea,' replied Aquila, who greatly

preferred the scholarly silence of the library to the frenzy of the race track and looked thoroughly out of place. 'But it may interest you to know that that giant obelisk was brought to Rome from Egypt by the emperor Caligula.'

Lucius barely heard him. 'They're going to crash if they're not careful!' he shouted.

Aquila's friend and fellow senator, Galerius Horatius Canio, leaned across Aquila to make himself heard to Lucius. 'They're all trying to position themselves close to the spina,' he explained. 'It's the best place to be. Your brother must hold his nerve, and his position, and not be crowded out. But watch out for the turns. That's where most of the crashes happen.' Canio was a jolly, round-faced man with a paunch discernible beneath the folds of his toga. He was visibly sweating under the hot September sun.

Lucius watched, gripped by the drama, as four of the chariots – Quin's included – vied for pole position closest to the spina. The horses' muzzles were flecked with foam and their eyes bulged manically while their drivers fought to inch ahead of their rivals. By the time they reached the turning post at the end of the spina, Quin was narrowly in the lead.

'He's done it! He's in front!'

'It's a long race,' cautioned Canio.

Lucius stared, heart in mouth, as his brother pulled his horses into a tight turn at high speed, only just avoiding a collision with the turning post. Meanwhile, a desperate tussle for third place between a Green and a Red charioteer led to the first accident of the afternoon. Green must have pushed Red too tightly against the turning post, for suddenly Red's chariot flipped onto its side. The Red driver tumbled out and was then pulled along the track by his panicked horses.

'Why doesn't he let go of the reins?' cried Lucius.

'He can't,' responded Senator Canio. 'He's wrapped them around his waist – the riders do that so they can use their body weight to control the horses. Now he must use his knife to free himself.'

Lucius watched open-mouthed as the rider was hauled painfully along the dusty track. But before he could cut himself free of the reins, he disappeared under the hooves of a team of horses coming up behind. Lucius caught a horrific glimpse of the rider being twisted and jerked about, then crushed beneath the horses' hooves and the wheels of the chariot. Red's mangled, bleeding body lay there on the sand until stretcher-bearers were able to dash onto the track and carry it away.

The other charioteers safely negotiated the turn and began racing once more along the straight. Quin had managed to maintain his position on the innermost part of the track, but was facing severe competition from a Blue charioteer, who was now neck-and-neck with him. The rivals urged their horses faster with cracks of their whips. They seemed entirely equal in speed and strength. On the second turn, Blue made his move: he turned more tightly than expected, straying into Quin's line and forcing Quin even closer to the turning post in order to avoid a collision. There was an audible crack, as Quin's axle hit the post's semicircular base. His chariot wobbled, and for a second Lucius was sure he would be upended and would share the gruesome fate of the Red charioteer. But somehow, Quin managed to keep his chariot balanced, and on they went. The wobble must have slowed or unnerved him, though, because Blue now edged in front.

The other charioteers soon followed around the turn. A bell sounded and one of the seven bronze dolphins suspended above the turning post lowered its head, marking the completion of the first lap. The race settled into a steadier pattern on the second lap, with Blue in the lead, Quin in second place, Green in third and the rest strung out behind. Green was gaining on Quin, though, and it didn't take Lucius long to figure out why: as Quin passed beneath Lucius's seat for the second time, he noticed that his brother's chariot wheel – the one whose axle had grazed the turning post – was wobbling very slightly, and this was slowing him down. Yet Quin was stubbornly resisting Green's attacks, skilfully cutting him off every time he tried to edge past him on the inside.

'Quintus is displaying admirable perseverence and skill,' commented Canio, who was a seasoned racegoer, 'but I fear he won't be able to hold off the challenge from Bassus for long.'

21

The battle between Quin and Bassus for second place was obsessing everyone, to judge from the increasing noise levels. The stadium had become a billowing sea of green and white banners as supporters of the rival teams tried to out-shout each other.

Shortly after the fourth bronze dolphin had lowered its head, there was another crash, and this time it was a big one. A representative of the Greens, under pressure from a White, lost control and smashed his chariot against the spina. The pursuing White was unable to swerve in time and ploughed straight into the upended chariot, killing the Green charioteer. Then a Blue, just behind him, crashed into the wreckage. This caused a domino effect, and in the blink of an eye five chariots had crashed out of the race. The accident happened right under Lucius's nose, so he was forced to witness, in sickening close-up, the deaths of five more charioteers, and perhaps twice that number of horses. The track beneath him looked like a battlefield, strewn with blood-soaked men and twitching, frightened horses alongside the splintered remains of chariots.

'It's like a scene from Cannae,' murmured a pale-faced Aquila.

Lucius nodded, understanding his father immediately. The Battle of Cannae, as every schoolboy knew, had taken place nearly 300 years earlier, during the war against Hannibal of Carthage. It was, by common consent, the worst defeat Rome had ever suffered. During the battle, the Roman cavalry had been annihilated by Hannibal's horsemen.

The slaves who were employed to keep the track clear during races now had the dangerous task of removing the bodies and the wreckage while the race continued around them. A couple of slaves were a little slow at evading oncoming chariots, and they, too, lost their lives.

When Quin swerved to avoid the wreckage, Bassus took the opportunity to overtake, pushing Quin into third place. And, with his damaged wheel, it seemed he had little chance now of improving on this position.

'It looks as though your brother may have to settle for third,' said Canio. 'Still, not too bad for a boy who's only been racing for a year.'

Once he was past Quin, Bassus rapidly closed in on his next target, the Blue charioteer who had been leading the field since the second lap. As the final lap commenced, the two became locked in a tight contest, while Quin himself came under pressure from the fourth-placed Red charioteer, who was steadily overtaking him on the outside.

So, the crowd's attention became split between two battles: between Blue and Green for first place, and between White and Red for third. Fights broke out between rival fans, as excitement spiralled into hysteria. Then Blue and Green turned into the final straight and two things happened that changed the race completely.

First, Red's whip, through freakish mischance (or so he later claimed), became entangled around Quin's loose wheel, pulling it clean off the axle. After the race, the White team accused the Red charioteer of deliberate sabotage – an act of desperation, because he knew he wasn't going to catch Quin.

Just as Quin appeared to be tumbling out of the race, everyone's attention was diverted towards an even more dramatic event: Blue and Green, with scarcely a sesterce's* width separating them, seemed about to cross the finish line together, when an object came flying onto the track from the Blue section of the crowd. Lucius thought it looked like a curse amulet, studded with nails. Whatever it was, it frightened Green's outermost horse, causing it to rear. Green lost control. His chariot skidded and collided with Blue's, sending both tumbling over and over. The horses continued to gallop, dragging their fallen riders along the ground. The men had to use the knives they kept in their belts to free themselves. Luckily, both managed to escape from the track before they got trampled.

Quin later claimed it was the reflexes he'd acquired during his days as a gladiator that had saved him when his chariot wheel fell off. Not many could say exactly how he did it, as most were watching the crash between Blue and Green at the time, but as soon as Quin felt himself tipping over, he made a flying leap. It took him clear out of the chariot, and he managed to sink

---

* *sesterce: a brass coin about 30 mm or so in diameter.*

his fingers into the hindquarters of the horse directly in front of him, just as his chariot tumbled away. So fast were they going that the skin was instantly ripped from his toes and the tops of his feet as he was dragged along the gritty surface of the track.

Through sheer force of will and upper-body strength, Quin was able to clamber up onto the horse's back. When they saw him standing atop the horse, still controlling all four animals with the reins, the White supporters rose as one and roared their appreciation. Placing his feet akimbo for balance, Quin leaned hard to his left just in time to pull the horses around the final turn. With their lightened load, Quin's horses were easily able to outpace Red's, and thus it was Quin who was first across the finish line.

Quin remained on his feet on top of the horse during his lap of honour, one arm held aloft in triumph. The White supporters were ecstatic, and grudging applause could even be heard coming from the Blue and Green sections of the crowd for this unorthodox yet astonishing feat of athleticism. Lucius cheered as loudly and passionately as anyone in the senatorial seats. Aquila smiled and applauded, while Canio was shaking his head. 'I've never seen anything like it,' he muttered. 'Sadly, I don't think it'll be allowed to stand.'

Meanwhile, the stewards of the Circus Maximus consulted urgently with the sponsor, Glabrio, and a decision was soon announced: as this was a chariot race, the winner had to be riding a chariot when crossing the finishing line. Therefore, the winner of the race was… Lepontus for the Red team.

This decision prompted a chorus of boos from the White supporters, and an immediate protest from their official representatives, who declared Lepontus a cheat and a scoundrel who should be disqualified, not honoured. What kind of precedent did this set? Did they actually want to encourage riders to pull the wheels off their opponents' chariots? Another hasty round of consultations ensued, and the victory palm was finally awarded to a member of the Green team named Torquatus, who had been next across the line after Quin and Lepontus.

By the time this announcement was made, Quin had long since departed the track. He neither knew nor cared what the judges decided. For him, racing, like fighting, was all about the glory and intensity of the action itself – the result was of little importance.

PART ONE

DEATH OF AN EMPEROR

CHAPTER I

12 SEPTEMBER

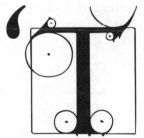'There's nothing like the feeling of living from second to second,' Quin explained to Lucius, 'surrendering yourself to Neptune, the god of our noble sport. You can keep all your history and philosophy, brother. They'll never take you to the essence of what life's about so well as racing chariots.'

'They'll never cut your feet to ribbons either,' observed Lucius drily.

They were in the all-too-familiar setting of a medical room – Quin seemed to spend a lot of time in such places. This one was part of the stadium complex and dedicated to treating injured charioteers. Quin was sitting on a bench, having his feet cleaned and bandaged by Glaukos, the White team's surgeon. Lucius had come here directly after the race, preferring to be with Quin rather than listen to his father and Canio gossiping with their senatorial colleagues in the stands. He couldn't help staring at the many scars on his brother's muscular torso, the legacy of his short, yet violent career as gladiator, bestiarius and now charioteer.

'This is the life,' sighed Quin. His blue eyes sparkled happily. 'All the drama and excitement of the gladiatorial arena – and nobody has to get killed.'

'Nine people died today,' Lucius pointed out.

'Yeah, well – accidents happen,' shrugged Quin. 'But the deaths were incidental – they weren't part of the entertainment.'

'So why can't they make it safer?' Lucius asked.

'If it was safe, no one would want to come and watch.'

'And I'd be out of a job,' muttered Glaukos.

Aquila came in, followed by Canio.

'Congratulations, Quintus,' said Aquila stiffly. Lucius had hoped that Quin's heroics this afternoon might have softened Aquila's antipathy towards his son's chosen sport – but there was no trace of a smile on his face.

'You were the moral victor today, young sir,' Canio declared. 'Everyone's saying so.'

'Which is another way of saying that I wasn't the actual victor,' chuckled Quin.

'Sadly not,' said Canio, 'though you may have

accidentally invented a new sport. When your father and I left the stadium, the intermission acrobats were already mimicking your standing-on-horseback riding style. It's becoming quite a hit.'

'Pleased to hear it!' said Quin. 'So, Father, have I succeeded in opening your eyes to the joys of chariot racing?'

Aquila frowned and shook his head. He was tall, like his elder son, but with a leaner frame. His years of study had left him with a slight stoop and the permanent squint of a man with poor eyesight. 'To be frank with you, I was quite baffled by the whole thing. How all those thousands of people can get so worked up at the sight of men driving chariots around in circles is a mystery to me. If it was about the swiftness of the horses or the skill of the charioteers, that would be one thing. But as far as I can tell, their love affair is with a certain bit of coloured cloth. So long as a man wearing their favoured colour crosses the line before every other man, they're happy. It's quite ludicrous, Quintus, and it's high time you put aside these childish pursuits and began taking life more seriously.'

His words brought a flush of anger to Quin's cheeks. 'These childish pursuits, as you call them, are all I ever want to do,' he retorted. 'You know I have no interest in your boring world of politics and debate.'

Lucius cringed. This was a common argument between the two of them at home, and he didn't relish it being replayed here in front of Canio and Glaukos.

'Remember who you are, Quintus,' said Aquila. 'You're a Valerius, a member of a venerable, aristocratic family with ancestors that can be traced back to –'

'To the early Republic,* I know,' interrupted Quin. 'And so what? When you left us, we lost everything. And what did our venerable, aristocratic name count for then? Nothing! It didn't buy us food or put a roof over our heads. The only practical path in life is to be true to yourself, and to survive on your merits – not on your name.'

'He's starting to sound like one of those Cynic philosophers,'** chuckled Canio.

But Aquila wasn't amused. 'I've indulged your fantasies for too long, Quintus. I came today because you begged me to, but I shall never set foot in the Circus Maximus again, and neither shall you. You must give up chariot racing immediately, or I will cut off your allowance, and you can find somewhere else to live.'

Quin's jaw dropped open in shock. 'But Father, do you have any idea how much a charioteer earns? Are you going to cast me back into poverty?'

Aquila was unmoved. 'You said you wished to survive on your merits, not on your name. Well, that's exactly what you'll have to do.'

---

* *Republic: Rome became a republic – a state with an elected government – around 509 BC. In 27 BC, Augustus became the first emperor of Rome, and the republic ended. So Lucius's family is nearly 600 years old.*

** *Cynic philosophers: ancient Greek scholars who believed in leading a simple and virtuous life, without ambitions or worldly goods.*

Before Quin could think of a response to this, Aquila's secretary, a freedman* named Timon, entered. He was a thin man with a quick, nervous manner. 'Patrone,** there is someone outside who wishes to speak with you.'

'If it's a client, tell him to come along tomorrow morning for the salutatio,'*** snapped Aquila. 'He can wait his turn along with everyone else.'

Timon hesitated. 'It's not a client, sir. He says the matter is urgent. It concerns...' Glancing around at the others in the room, the secretary broke off. He moved closer to Aquila and whispered something in his ear.

Aquila paled. His forehead creased in alarm. 'In that case,' he said, 'show him in.'

The man who entered on Timon's ushering seemed ancient, yet somehow ageless. His wiry brown body was clothed in a Greek-style himation – a large cloth draped over his left shoulder and about his body – the typical attire of a wandering philosopher or mystic. He had a wrinkled face, a thick grey beard and topaz eyes that seemed to glitter with mysterious secrets. On seeing him, the surgeon Glaukos, who had just finished bandaging Quin, gasped and rose to his feet.

---

* *freedman: an ex-slave who has been set free (manumitted) by his master or mistress as a reward for good service.*

** *Patrone: master, protector.*

*** *client: a person who receives or hopes for support or favours from an important Roman citizen; salutatio: a morning visit paid by a client to his patron.*

'Greetings, Senators, young men,' said the old man. He spoke with an accent of the east, which Lucius could not identify.

'Salve!'* said Aquila. 'I understand you have some information for us. But first, please tell us who you are.'

'He is Apollonius of Tyana,'** said Glaukos in awed tones. 'I have seen you before, oh prophet! Twenty years ago, when I was a young man living in Ephesus, I heard you foretell the great fire of Rome, the death of Nero and other cataclysmic events.' He turned to Aquila. 'Listen to what he has to say, I beg of you, sir. He has astonishing powers.'

'I am but a humble philosopher,' said the man.

'You are far more than that,' asserted Aquila. 'I have read of your miraculous feats of prediction, Apollonius.'

The old man inclined his head modestly. 'Sometimes the gods favour me with glimpses of things to come… I experienced one such vision this morning.'

'About the emperor?'

Apollonius nodded. 'He will die on the Ides of September.'***

'What?' cried Quin.

---

* *Salve: greetings!*
** *Apollonius of Tyana: a real-life philosopher of the 1st century AD. Many stories are told about his marvellous powers, but little is known about him for real.*
*** *Ides of September: the 15th of September.*

36

Lucius felt a jolt course through his body. The Ides of September were tomorrow.

'Impossible!' said Canio. 'Our emperor is young and in excellent health.'

'Then it can only mean one thing,' said Glaukos with a shudder.

A frightened silence filled the room.

'Are you suggesting that someone will kill him?' Aquila demanded.

'He will die,' answered Apollonius, 'in the same way that Odysseus is said to have died, for they say that he, too, met his death by the sea.'

'What in Hades* does that mean?' Canio thundered. 'Will he drown?'

Apollonius did not reply. He simply bowed and departed the room. 'Get after him, Timon,' shouted Aquila. 'Bring him back here. We haven't finished with our questions.'

Timon ran out. He returned a few moments later, a puzzled look on his face. 'I have searched everywhere, sir. I can't understand how a man as old as that could have moved so fast. It's as if he's vanished into the air.'

'It does not surprise me,' said Glaukos, packing away his medical tools. 'Many are the tales I've heard of Apollonius of Tyana – they say he can restore life to the dead, exorcise evil spirits and cure whole cities of plague. For such a man, vanishing should be a simple enough trick.'

* *Hades: the Roman underworld, the abode of the dead.*

'I've heard those tales, too,' said Aquila, 'and most of them I'm sure are purest fantasy. Yet no man acquires such a reputation for nothing.'

Canio stared at Aquila. 'You mean you're going to take the ravings of this street prophet seriously?'

'I don't think we have any choice,' replied Aquila. 'Though I find his suggestion that the emperor will meet his death by the sea somewhat perplexing. After all, Titus left for his family villa at Aquae Cutiliae in Sabinium* earlier today, and that's nowhere near the sea.'

'Which only proves the man's a charlatan,' said Canio.

Aquila seemed to consider this for a moment, then shook his head. 'If there's even the remotest possibility that our emperor is in danger, it's my duty to report it. Timon, summon the litter bearers, and send a message to the ostler on the Via Salaria.** I want his fastest travelling chariot to be ready and waiting for me there.'

'Wait!' said Canio. 'You mean you're actually going in person to the emperor's private villa, without an invitation? Why not send a messenger?'

'Messages can be intercepted,' said Aquila. 'And if there's a conspiracy against Titus, it may well involve

---

* *Aquae Cutiliae: a hot spring about 65 km northeast of Rome; Sabinium: the territory of the Sabines, a neighbouring people who became part of the Roman state in ancient times.*

** *The Via Salaria (Latin for 'salt road') runs northeast from Rome to the Adriatic coast, passing through Reate and Aquae Cutiliae. Litter: a couch or chair carried on poles. Ostler: a groom who looks after horses.*

the people around him. The only way I can be sure that my warning will get through is to deliver it myself.'

Canio nodded thoughtfully. 'Aquae Cutiliae is forty-five miles away.* You won't get there tonight.'

'I'll journey through the night.' He turned to Timon. 'Go! Quickly!' Timon went.

'Let me go, too, Father,' said Quin.

'And me!' said Lucius.

Aquila smiled and shook his head. 'I appreciate the offer, boys, but if there are assassins around, I don't want either of you anywhere near the scene.'

'The roads can be dangerous at night, Father,' said Lucius. 'At least take a mounted escort.'

'You forget,' said Aquila, 'I survived eleven months on my own, with little more than my wits to protect me. I assure you I'll be fine.' The litter bearers arrived and he climbed aboard.

Meanwhile, Canio had summoned his own litter. Before Aquila left, the portly senator parted his curtain. 'I'll not let you go on this fool's errand alone, old friend. I'll meet you at the start of the Via Salaria at hora decima.** We'll travel together.'

Aquila eyed Canio's large girth dubiously. 'In that case, we may need a bigger carriage.' Then he nodded. 'Very well, then.' He raised his hand. 'Avete!*** See you all soon.'

* *A Roman mile was 1,000 paces, which equates to 1,481 metres.*
** *hora decima: the tenth hour of the day – about 4 p.m.*
*** *Avete: farewell.*

CHAPTER II

14 SEPTEMBER

ucius stood on the terrace of the family mansion, perched on the upper slopes of the Esquiline Hill. By his side was his loyal dog Argos. He was a large brown Molossus,* sitting erect with ears alert and tongue lolling. Lucius stroked the fur on his head, taking comfort from the dog's warmth and presence as he gazed out across the city. It was a view he had known since childhood, though it had changed over the years – as had his feelings about it. It seemed that wherever he looked these days, there lay an unpleasant memory ready to stab at his heart.

Dominating the view to the south, on what had once been a lake, stood the vast, white Flavian

---

Molossus: a large, heavy breed of dog, often used as a guard dog.

Amphitheatre.* It appeared almost to float in the mid-morning haze with the innocent grace of a swan. Yet he could never look at it without hearing again the terrified screams of the animals caged in its dungeons, or reliving the sight of their slaughter on its blood-soaked sands.

Further north, beyond the marble temples and basilicas of the Forum,** lay the densely packed tenements of the Suburra district. Once he'd regarded that quarter with wide-eyed curiosity, wondering how people could survive in its crowded, stinking streets without slaves or running water. Now he no longer had to wonder. For eleven long months, during the period of his father's exile, Lucius and his family had endured a squalid existence there – it was an experience he would never forget.

Further on, between the Capitoline and Palatine Hills, lay the run-down area called the Velabrum, and the sight of its hazy rooftops brought more sad memories. It was in one of those insulae*** that Agathon, Lucius's long-time friend and tutor, had perished in the fire that burned through Rome last year. Argos had loved Agathon – the dog had never been the same since he died.

* *Flavian Amphitheatre: a huge arena for gladiatorial combat and other entertainments, known today as the Colosseum. At the time of our story it was almost brand-new.*

** *basilicas: large public halls used for business meetings; Forum: the main marketplace in Rome, which was also the place where citizens met to discuss business.*

*** *insulae: multistorey apartment blocks.*

Even the opulent Palatine, with its red-tiled rooftops and colonnaded terraces, could give Lucius no solace – for his wicked uncle Ravilla, whose scheming had so nearly robbed him of his father, had lived there.

'Where is Father?' Lucius suddenly wondered. Argos uttered a brief whine, sensing his master's anxiety. Lucius had expected his father's return from Aquae Cutiliae this morning. He was impatient for news. Had Apollonius been right about a plot against the emperor?

The day was almost too quiet. The city spread out beneath him seemed strangely placid and still, as if lost in some kind of reverie. The only sounds were the splash of a nearby fountain and the distant cry of vultures above the city necropolis* near the Esquiline Gate.

And then, with shocking abruptness, the calm was shattered by a long, shrill scream.

Lucius whirled around as Philaenis, a kitchen slave, blundered onto the terrace. Fruit from the basket she was carrying tipped and rolled all over the floor. Argos, made nervous by the commotion, began to bark.

'Oh, Master Lucius!' Philaenis cried. 'It's terrible! Have you heard? The emperor – our beloved emperor. He's dead!'

It was as though a bubble had burst – a spell had been broken. The house, the entire city, was violently

---

* *necropolis. a burial ground with fine monuments, built outside the city gates. The word means 'city of the dead' in Greek.*

shaken from its slumber. A faint howling rose up on the breeze. It sounded like the weeping of thousands.

Over the next hour, Lucius watched as streams of people began making their way down a steep, winding spur of the Esquiline and along the Via Sacra towards the Forum, the city's traditional gathering place at times of triumph and catastrophe. Titus was dead! He had reigned for just two years and two months, yet he was perhaps the most beloved emperor since the very first, the divine Augustus.

All that morning and on into the afternoon, reports, rumours and wild speculation swirled around the streets and squares, the markets and the bath-houses, before being delivered to the hilltop mansions of the wealthy by their clients, freedmen and slaves.

He died in his sleep.
He died of an insect bite.
He was murdered.
He was killed by his brother Domitian.
The Praetorian guards* are in revolt.
The legions are on the march.
Domitian is in hiding.
Domitian is dead.
Domitian is emperor.

* *Praetorian guards: the emperor's bodyguard.*

Lucius saw and felt the fear and panic in the city. He waited for news of his father, but none came. Oh, what had happened out there in Aquae Cutiliae? Why had they let Father go? And what did the future now hold for Rome? Lucius was too young to remember the bloody civil war that had followed Emperor Nero's downfall fourteen years earlier – the so-called Year of Four Emperors – but his father had often recalled it with a shudder. The death of an emperor was always a time of chaos and uncertainty, of plots and palace coups. He prayed that Domitian, Titus's brother, was indeed alive and that imperial power could pass peacefully to him. Most of all, he prayed that his father was alive and would come back soon.

The clock slave had called the ninth hour of the day[*] by the time they received official confirmation of Titus's death. A colleague of Aquila's by the name of Julianus Novius Dio arrived at their house from the Senate. The family gathered in the atrium[**] to hear what he had to say. To their disappointment, Dio had heard nothing of Aquila – was not even aware he'd been at the emperor's villa.

'Titus died of a fever,' Dio informed them. 'It took him quite suddenly on the night he arrived at his villa. By the following afternoon he was dead. Any stories you've heard of foul play are malicious lies. It was a malady, perhaps a recurrence of an old illness he'd

* ninth hour of the day: about 3 p.m.
** atrium: the entrance courtyard of a Roman house, where guests were received.

45

picked up during his campaigning days in the east. His brother Domitian was with him to the end, after which he made haste to the Castra Praetoria – the camp of the Praetorian guards outside Rome – where he was immediately proclaimed emperor. His prompt action appears to have forestalled any potential for unrest. This morning, the Senate confirmed Domitian's accession, granting him the powers of the imperium and the tribunate, the office of Pontifex Maximus and the titles of Augustus and Pater Patriae.'*

'What does all that mean?' asked Valeria, who was accompanied as always by her pet chimpanzee, Simio.

'It means he's the new top man,' said Quin.

After Dio left, they waited in tense, fidgety silence for Aquila's return. Even Simio's attempt to juggle figs and catch them in his mouth failed to lift the mood.

'Your father always was the most impetuous of men,' tutted Caecilia, the children's mother. 'Fancy flying off like that on an overnight journey without any sort of protective escort. He and Canio were probably ambushed by robbers on the road. I doubt they even made it to the emperor's villa.'

'He was right to go, though, wasn't he?' said Lucius,

---

* *imperium: the right to rule; tribunate: the office of tribune (an official who, by law, could not be harmed); Pontifex Maximus, Augustus, Pater Patriae: these are all official titles of the Roman emperor.*

annoyed by the way his mother was always quick to find fault with Aquila. 'Titus died on the Ides, just as Apollonius predicted. Father was trying to save the emperor!'

'A fat lot of good it did,' muttered Caecilia. 'He should have sent a messenger, as any sensible man would. But no! He had to play the hero.'

'Father is alive,' said Valeria quietly but firmly.

'How can you possibly know that?' her mother challenged her.

'Because Simio is calm,' she said, smiling serenely at her pet as he played with a set of marble latrunculi* pieces while nibbling on a fig. 'Simio always knows when a member of the family is in danger.'

The sun was casting its last rays over the temple roofs of the Capitoline Hill when Aquila finally returned. Lucius, Quin and Valeria raced into the vestibule to greet him, with Caecilia following on at a more dignified pace.

'I'm so happy to see you, Father,' wept Valeria as she hugged him. 'What took you so long? You must tell us everything. And don't leave out a single detail!'

Aquila, looking pale and weary, managed a grim smile. 'Patience, Valeria. Will you at least give me a chance for a wash and a change of toga?'

latrunculi: a Roman board game.

At dinner, Aquila refused to be drawn on what had occurred at Aquae Cutiliae. 'We'll talk about that later,' he said, with a glance at the serving boy.

So, thought Lucius, whatever news he had was too sensitive to be revealed in front of the slaves. Perhaps there was more to the story of Titus's death than Dio had divulged.

Over a simple meal of roast pork with boiled carrots and asparagus (which Valeria insisted on smothering in cheap garum sauce, as was her way), Aquila spoke with regret of the passing of Titus. 'I truly believed we were entering a glorious era,' he said. 'The emperor was young and full of vigour – he could have lived another thirty years. And he cared deeply for his people, as shown by his generous donations of aid for the victims of Vesuvius and the fire in Rome.'

'There is no reason to believe his brother will be any worse,' said Caecilia.

'No, of course not,' said Aquila. 'Only Domitian appears to have been cut from a different kind of cloth. I have met both men on occasion over the years, and while Titus was always courteous and friendly, Domitian was sullen and ill-tempered. I fear he may not be the emperor Titus was. We know he publicly objected to Titus's succession two years ago, believing their father had wanted them to rule jointly. That speaks to me of a man motivated more by personal ambition than by a sense of civic duty. But you're right, my dear. We shouldn't rush to judgement, and I hope I am proved wrong.' Aquila summoned a slave to refill his wine cup. 'Enough about politics,' he said, taking a swig. 'The death of our emperor has also set me thinking about another matter: namely, my own mortality.'

'Father!' cried Valeria. 'You're not planning to die, too, are you?'

Aquila laughed. 'Not for a long time, I hope. Still, I'm not going to live forever and I want to be sure that the family is in good hands after I'm gone. You, Quintus, as my elder son, will one day be head of this household and we need to begin our preparations for that. Next year you will give up your boyish toga praetexta and don the plain white toga virilis, signifying that you are ready to take on the responsibilities of manhood. In due course, I would like you to embark on the cursus honorum – the career path for all men of our rank – starting with ten years of service as a tribune.'

Quin angrily slammed down the drinking vessel he'd been holding.

'Is there something you wish to say?' Aquila calmly enquired.

Lucius observed his brother's flushed cheeks, and felt sorry for him. All Quin desired was to go on racing chariots, but to do that he'd have to give up everything – his name, his inheritance, his home here on the Esquiline. He'd done it once before, of course, when he became a gladiator, but then it had been out of necessity.

'No, Father,' sighed Quin. 'I have nothing to say.'

After dinner, they gathered in the tablinum – Aquila's private study. It was an austere, dimly lit chamber, its walls lined with pigeonholes containing piles of letters and accounts. Hollow-eyed, waxen death masks of the family's ancestors stared from their niches.

Aquila dismissed the slaves and gave instructions that they weren't to be disturbed. Then he closed the door and turned to address his family. His first words were truly shocking.

'I must inform you that Titus was murdered.'

'What?' cried Quin and Lucius together.

'Senator Dio told us he died of a fever,' said Valeria.

'That is what everyone believes,' nodded Aquila. 'I know different. So does Canio.'

'Murdered by whom?' asked Lucius. 'Not... not Domitian?' He was thinking of his father's words earlier.

Aquila sighed and scratched his head. 'I hope not, but who can say? He wasn't directly involved. There was someone else...'

They waited for him to go on. He paced the floor for a while. 'I can't tell you who,' he said finally. 'Not yet. Such knowledge could endanger you all. I plan to make a speech before the Senate tomorrow. After that, once it's public knowledge, it will be safe for you to be told everything. For now, what I can say is that old Apollonius was correct in his prediction. If you remember, he said that Titus would meet his death "by the sea", and we all assumed he meant drowning. In fact, the emperor was killed by something fished from the sea – namely, a sea-hare.'

'What's a sea-hare?' asked Valeria.

'It's a kind of marine slug, and one of the late emperor's favourite dishes. Unfortunately, this one was poisoned.'

'How can you know that?' asked Caecilia with a sceptical note in her voice.

Aquila sat down behind his desk and pressed his fists to his cheeks. He grimaced, as if the burden of the terrible knowledge he was carrying was giving him physical pain. After a while, he said: 'As Titus lay dying, one of his entourage slipped away from his bedside. On a whim, Canio and I followed him, but we lost him in the unfamiliar corridors of the villa. We were about to return to the emperor when we heard an agonised cry coming from the kitchen. We rushed in to find the cook, Bibulus, knifed through the chest. Before he died, he managed to whisper to us that the man, the one we'd followed, had forced him to poison the fish, or see his own family killed. And now that same man had returned to silence Bibulus.'

'And only you and Canio know about this?' asked Quin.

'Of those still alive, yes,' said Aquila bleakly. 'The emperor also guessed, but by then it was too late. We were all gathered there around his bedside. I'll never forget the moment. Suddenly, he fixed his murderer with that famous steel-blue gaze and said: "I have made but one mistake." Those were his last words... His mistake was to trust this man.'

Aquila rose to his feet. 'Now I must ask you all to leave me so that I can work on my speech to the Senate.'

'You cannot give that speech,' said Caecilia. Lucius saw his mother's hands were shaking.

'My dear, it is my duty to inform the Senate of this monstrous act. Our emperor was killed. Do you not agree this is something the people ought to know about?'

'Remember what you said earlier, husband,' Caecilia persisted. 'This is a new era now. Domitian is not like Titus. If the official story is that Titus died of a fever, then it would be dangerous to say otherwise. Dangerous for you, dangerous for your family.'

After the children had retired to bed, Lucius lay awake in his room listening to his parents arguing. He couldn't make out their words, but the violence of their disagreement was clear from the steady rise in the pitch and volume of their voices. Lucius could see both their points of view. Aquila was right that the murder of the emperor ought to be exposed. On the other hand, what if Domitian was behind the murder? As emperor he now wielded supreme power and would be a very dangerous man to cross. It seemed as though his father was playing with fire.

At some stage, shortly after the clock slave had called the third watch of the night,* there came a knock at his door.

'Come in,' he hissed, expecting that Valeria had come to discuss their parents' fight. Instead, his mother entered. In the guttering light of the lamp she was carrying, he saw that her face, normally smooth as marble, was creased with nerves. She looked as though she'd been crying.

'Get up, Lucius,' she whispered. 'We're leaving.'

'Leaving? What do you mean?'

'You, me, Quintus and Valeria. We're leaving this house now. Your father refuses to see reason. I've tried to persuade him, but he's set upon a course of action that can only end in calamity for all of us. Our only chance is to flee.'

'Flee where?'

'I have a friend,' she said, 'a powerful friend. He will protect us. We must go there now, before your father wakes and tries to stop us.'

* *third watch of the night: midnight.*

Lucius hesitated. 'Father wants to tell people the truth. What's wrong with that?'

'The truth…,' sighed Caecilia as she sat down on the bed. 'The truth, my darling, is whatever those in power say it is. If they tell us that Titus died of a fever, then Titus died of a fever. That is the truth. You have to understand that, Lucius, if you want to survive in this world.'

Something stirred within him when she said this. He was grateful to his mother for showing him which way his heart lay. 'If what you say is true, then maybe I don't want to survive,' he said through gritted teeth.

She gripped his hands in hers. 'Come, now. No more arguing. Get dressed.'

Lucius pulled his hands free and gathered the bedclothes around him protectively. 'I'm not going, Mother. I'd sooner die.'

Fresh tears trickled down his mother's cheeks as she rose to her feet. 'Just like your father,' she moaned. 'Principled to the point of stupidity.' She went to the door.

'What about Quin and Val?' he asked.

She pursed her lips. 'Unfortunately, they're being just as foolish and stubborn as you.'

'Please stay, Mother,' he pleaded.

She shook her head sadly. 'Take care, my son. I'll send for you in the morning – after Aquila has left for the Senate House. I pray that you'll have come to your senses by then.'

CHAPTER III

15 SEPTEMBER

aster Lucius.' The voice was soft, yet urgent. Lucius stirred in his bed and opened his eyes. He recognised the slave boy standing over him as his father's valet.

'What is it, Vedrix?'

'It's the master, sir. We've knocked on his bedroom door, but he won't answer. The mistress left the house last night, so we couldn't call her. So Tullas, the night guard, told me to come and fetch you and Master Quintus.'

Lucius leapt out of bed, his stomach suddenly tight with horrid foreboding. He ran out of his room and along the corridor to his father's bedroom, with Vedrix trailing in his wake.

Tullas was waiting there outside the door, along with young Micon, ready with razor and bowl for the master's morning shave. Lucius shouldered his way past them and knocked loudly on the door. 'Father!'

No reply.

'What's going on?' yawned a sleepy-eyed Quin, emerging from his bedroom.

Lucius ignored him and pushed open the door.

Shafts of peach-coloured early-morning light slanted through the single window and illuminated the bed. Aquila lay there on his back amid a jumble of sheets. His eyes were open and he appeared to be staring at the ceiling. Blood covered the sheets.

Lucius ran to him. When he saw the knife sticking out of his father's chest, his knees buckled and he collapsed to the floor.

'Father! No!'

He clutched at Aquila's outstretched hand and held it to his cheek. It was soft and cool, like the finest parchment. From somewhere above he heard a slave cry out, and his brother's throaty gasp. He heard echoing shouts, screams and running footsteps as the news began to spread around the house. He felt people moving around him, worried voices asking questions, but Lucius couldn't move or speak, couldn't let go of his father's hand. He held on to it tight, determined never to let go. His mind spun back to a bright June day fifteen months earlier – his father's return from exile. He had looked so lean and bronzed after his months in the countryside. Lucius recalled the feel of his father's strong hands around his shoulders, the warm sunshine of his smile, the connection between them, deep beyond words, which had always been there, always would…

The reverie was broken by the sound of sobbing. Val was lying in a heap on the floor, crying her eyes out. Quin was issuing urgent instructions to others in the room: 'Summon the city prefect! Guard all the doors and windows! The killer may still be in the house!'

Lucius realised he was no longer holding on to his father's hand. He tried to grab it again, but Quin pushed his arm away.

'Leave it!' he said. 'He's dead! Try and get up now.'

Lucius tried to get up, but couldn't. Quin's terrible words kept pressing down on his mind, crushing him with their cold weight like slabs of marble: HE'S DEAD. FATHER'S DEAD.

'Oh, Lucius. I can't believe this. I – I…' He felt Val hugging him, her hot breath against his cheek. He wanted to comfort her, but he had no words – none that would make sense. Where were the slaves? Where was Nicia? She should take his sister away from here, give her a soothing drink.

Val was babbling. 'Who would do this, Lucius? Who? Tell me! Oh, Mother was right. Father should never have got involved. How I hate this world. I wish I could die! Oh, Father! Father!' She collapsed into another bout of sobbing.

'Nicia!' he bellowed.

'She's not here,' said Quin. The room was a lot emptier now. Quin was standing there looking down at them. 'She's been confined to her quarters, along with all the other slaves. I've asked Father's clients and freedmen to guard them – they were all here for the salutatio. I've given orders that no slave be allowed to move from there until the city prefect arrives. For now, everyone is a suspect. I've also dispatched a messenger to Mother, telling her what's happened.'

He touched Aquila's cheek. Lucius could see the shake in his brother's hand. He was trying desperately to be strong – to stay in control of his emotions.

'Father...' Quin's voice cracked. 'His flesh is...' He cleared his throat and tried again. 'Rigor mortis has not yet set in. He can't have died long ago. Tullas swears no one came in through the bedroom door during the night.'

Lucius craned his neck towards the window behind him – the only other means of access. The shutter was open, but perhaps that wasn't surprising on such a warm night. Val was still clinging to him and quietly sobbing. He gently released himself from her and rose to his feet. Catching sight of his father again, he staggered and nearly fell back to the floor. The knife's blade was almost fully buried in his chest. Horrible!

'Do we have to leave him like this?' he asked.

Quin nodded. 'The investigators will need to see exactly how he died.'

Lucius thought he was going to vomit. He took a deep breath and gripped the footboard of the bed hard. When the feeling had passed, he walked over to the window and examined it. Immediately he saw something wrong. 'The shutter's been forced open,' he said.

Quin came over, and Lucius pointed out the splintered wood around the bolt. The window opened onto a red-tiled roof that overhung a row of columns – one side of a peristyle* that surrounded the garden. Outside, the fountain tinkled, flies buzzed – a normal day. Lucius choked back another wave of despair.

'One of the tiles is dislodged,' Quin pointed out. 'This is definitely how the murderer got in.'

There was a hesitant knock on the door. Quin turned and went to open it.

A freedwoman named Theodora was cowering there, her cheeks stained with tears. 'I'm so sorry,' she said, 'but the, er – the city prefect's arrived, along with about a dozen troopers. They're in the atrium. What shall I do?'

'Send them up here,' said Quin. He glanced back at his sister, still crumpled by the bed. 'And when you've done that, please take care of Valeria.'

'Of – of course,' she said, casting a sympathetic glance at Val.

'Be strong, Theodora,' said Quin. 'She needs your help.' The woman nodded and rushed off.

* _peristyle: a covered walkway with columns._

Junius Plautus, the city prefect, was a small, sharp-eyed man, who looked to Lucius more like a rat-catcher than the city's chief law officer. It was reassuring, though, that nothing seemed likely to escape his notice. After introducing himself and expressing his condolences to Quin, Lucius and Valeria, Plautus immediately set about examining every corner of the room for potential clues. A couple of troopers loitered near the door.

'I congratulate you on your quick work in securing the house, Quintus Valerius,' he said as he worked. 'Thanks to you, not a single slave has escaped. One of my deputies is currently downstairs questioning them.' He bent close to examine the body. After taking a careful look at the knife and the wound, he ordered one of his men to cover the body with a blanket.

Theodora, meanwhile, helped Valeria to her feet. Quin asked Plautus if his sister could be excused.

'Of course,' muttered the lawman. 'I can always question her later... Now perhaps you young men would be so good as to describe to me the events of last night and this morning.'

As Theodora led her from the room, Valeria gave Lucius a hard stare and raised a discreet finger to her lips. He knew instantly what his sister meant: they should keep quiet about their parents' fight and

Aquila's planned speech to the Senate. He wasn't sure he agreed – surely the city prefect ought to be informed of the most likely motive for the murder if he was to have any chance of catching the killer. On the other hand, what if Caecilia was right and the killer had been acting on the orders of Domitian? If they disclosed their knowledge of Titus's murder to this government official, they might not even get out of this room alive.

It was hard for Lucius to think clearly – the reality of his father's death kept shocking him anew. It was like being struck again and again by a freezing-cold storm wave. But somewhere within all that pummelling grief, a hardness had stolen into Lucius's heart. He would avenge his father's murder, and to do that he must stay alive. If that meant lying, so be it.

Quin started to speak, but Lucius cut in: 'It was a quiet night,' he told Plautus. 'We heard nothing until we were awoken this morning…'

Quin met his eyes, and Lucius was relieved to see that his brother understood and agreed with what he was doing.

Plautus, who had been on his knees exploring under Aquila's bed, suddenly looked up. He was holding an object he'd found there – a stylus of the sort used to write on wax tablets. 'Was your father in the habit of writing in bed?' he asked.

Lucius and Quin swapped a nervous glance. 'Er, he may have been…' said Lucius.

Plautus was back under the bed searching. 'Strange that there's a stylus here, but no tablet…' He got to his feet and walked over to the window, tapping the stylus thoughtfully against his lip. Observing the broken shutter and the dislodged tile, he muttered: 'Someone broke in here, clearly…' He turned to one of the troopers. 'Petreius, go and check the columns below this window for any marks, will you? The intruder may have climbed one of them to reach this window.'

After the trooper had left, Plautus addressed Lucius and Quin. 'Perhaps the object of this exercise was theft, as well as murder. Might your father have been working on anything sensitive last night? Something secret, perhaps, that certain parties might not have wished to see made public?'

'Nothing he told us about,' said Quin hurriedly.

There were loud footsteps in the corridor and a burly trooper entered, manhandling one of the slaves. Lucius recognised him as Pavo, a house guard. He had an ugly bruise on his cheek.

'Sir,' said the trooper, 'I was interviewing this one and–'

'I told you to question them, not beat them up, Gavrus,' frowned Plautus.

'If you'll just let me explain, sir–'

'Your man didn't give me this, Mister Prefect Sir,' said Pavo, indicating his cheek. 'It was the intruder.'

Lucius felt his neck hairs prickle. Had Pavo actually seen his father's murderer?

'Go on,' said Plautus.

Pavo explained what had happened. 'It was the final watch of the night, sir – not long before dawn. I was standing in the portico* at the front of the house when I caught sight of this hooded figure clambering down the pillar from the roof. I grabbed him as soon as he reached the ground. I pulled at his tunic, ripping the fabric. But he had something in his hands. It was like a flat piece of wood, and he clobbered me in the face with it. Before I could recover, he was away.'

'This object he hit you with,' asked Plautus. 'Could it have been a wax tablet?'

Pavo nodded. 'Quite possibly, sir. I'm not sure. It happened so fast. Besides, I was distracted…'

'Did you see his face?' asked Lucius impatiently.

This elicited a sharp look from Plautus. 'Young sir, if you don't mind, I'll ask the questions.' He turned back to Pavo. 'Well? Did you?'

'No. His hood completely covered his head, sir. But I did see something. As I said, it quite distracted me.'

'What did you see?'

'Well, when I ripped open the front of his tunic, I caught sight of his chest – this was just before he struck me – I saw on his bare chest, clear in the moonlight, a tattoo.'

'Can you describe it?'

'Probably best if I draw it, sir.'

'Very good. Calvinus, fetch some writing materials.'

* portico: an entrance porch with columns.

The second trooper exited, returning a few moments later with a sheet of papyrus, a reed pen and an ink pot. They all gathered around to watch as Pavo started to draw.

A gasp forced its way out of Lucius's throat when he saw the design emerge. It was crudely executed but unmistakable: a kestrel with wings outstretched and tail fanned beneath, and an arrow through its heart.

Quin and Plautus looked at Lucius curiously.

'What do you know of this?' asked Plautus.

'It's the mark of the Spectre,' said Lucius.

'You mean Vespasian's notorious informer, Gaius Valerius Ravilla – your uncle?'

Lucius nodded.

'But Ravilla died more than a year ago...' Plautus picked up the papyrus and examined the drawing more closely. 'You're certain this is what you saw?' he asked Pavo.

'Absolutely, sir.'

'It was your father who exposed Ravilla, wasn't it?' Plautus asked Lucius.

'With a little help from us,' muttered Quin.

'Ravilla always hated our father,' said Lucius. 'He nearly killed him once when they were boys, but the call of a kestrel saved Father's life. I think that may have been the origin of that sign.'

'Fascinating,' breathed Plautus.

They were pondering all this when Petreius returned and made his report. 'Couldn't find anything, sir. No scuff marks on the columns, no torn ivy or trampled vegetation. The intruder can't have come up that way.'

'No,' said Plautus absently, still staring at the kestrel. 'The fellow must have come along the roof. We're looking at an extremely agile, strong and ruthless man – with some connection to the victim's dead brother.'

'Oh, and there's a visitor in the atrium, sir,' added Petreius. 'Says he has an urgent message for Quintus, Lucius and Valeria. From their mother.'

The young man waiting for them in the atrium wore a pristine white tunic with a crimson sash – the livery of a rich man's personal servant. He was tall and strong with dark-blond curls and blue eyes. Lucius thought there was something vaguely familiar about him, and he wondered where he might have seen him before. It took him a few moments to realise that he bore more than a passing resemblance to Quin.

The youth introduced himself as Ennius. 'Your mother wants you two and your sister to come with me now,' he said to Lucius and Quin.

It was tactless of him to ignore the city prefect.

'Now wait just a minute,' said Plautus, rising up on the balls of his feet as if trying to make himself bigger. 'I'm in the middle of an investigation here and no one's leaving this house until I'm finished.'

Ennius bowed his head apologetically. 'I'm sorry,

Prefect, I should have made myself clearer. This is not a request, it's an order, and it comes both from the children's mother and from her host, Marcus Acilius Glabrio.'

At the mention of the consul's name, Plautus shrank back to his previous stature. 'Ah, well that puts a slightly different complexion on things.'

So, Glabrio was the powerful man Caecilia had fled to last night. Lucius had had no idea she even moved in such elite circles.

Ennius handed him a scroll with Glabrio's seal on it. Plautus cracked it open and scanned the message. 'The consul says he has every faith in my abilities – how kind! And he gives me complete authority to carry out my investigation...' He allowed himself a smile, his ruffled feathers now soothed. 'So it appears I am obliged to let you three go. No matter. If I have any further questions, I'll know where to find you.'

'My master lives in a mansion on the Palatine Hill,' Ennius told Lucius and Quin. 'You will be safe there under his protection. He says you are welcome to remain as his guests for as long as you wish.'

Lucius was suddenly filled with despair at the thought of leaving their father and their home. 'I don't want to go,' he muttered.

'Your mother insists,' said Ennius. 'She said that as long as the killer's on the loose, you're all in great danger – especially you boys – that's why she wants you with her.'

'Why are we in danger?' asked Quin.

'Because the killer is bound to fear that you'll want to avenge your father – so he's highly likely to strike first... But don't worry: my master's house is very well protected. You will be safe there until the killer is caught.'

'But what about Father?' said Lucius. 'We can't just leave him.' He felt himself starting to cry; he closed his eyes and clenched his shaking jaw, knowing that once he started he wouldn't be able to stop.

'We need to prepare his body.'

Valeria's voice rang out across the atrium. They looked up to see her standing there on the upstairs balcony. She was pale, but her expression was determined, her eyes startlingly bright.

'You must wait for us,' she said to Ennius. 'We want do this properly. We must honour our father's shade.'

Valeria led her brothers into Aquila's bedroom. She removed the blanket. Fresh tears sprang from her eyes when she saw him. Her hand went to her mouth. Quin took the knife by its handle and drew it from his father's chest. Each of them took their turn to kiss their father. Lucius found a silver denarius and placed it in his mouth – payment for Charon the ferryman, who would convey his soul across the River Styx to the abode of the dead. He closed Aquila's eyes.

'I don't know the lamentation prayers,' sobbed Valeria. 'I wish Mother was here.'

Lucius hugged her. 'Don't worry, Val. Just say whatever comes naturally to you.'

She spoke slowly, hesitantly: 'Oh Father, I refuse to say that you are gone, that you are dead. It doesn't seem right to say it when I can feel you still, here in my heart. I can hear your voice, feel the brush of your fingers in my hair. You were, you always will be, my guiding light, my star. You are not dead, Father. Not to me. But I know… I know you must make a journey now. And I hope you don't feel alone. I trust you will find some like-minded friends. And books. You must have books!' She smiled sadly. 'One day, I will join you there, and you'll tell me everything. I'll insist upon it! Until then, you know I'll have you here in my heart. I hope you won't mind me talking to you from time to time…'

They were quiet for a while after that, each of them thinking in their different ways about the man who had meant everything to them. Then they undressed him. Valeria, with Theodora's help, washed her father, wiping away all traces of blood, then annointed him with perfumed oil. After dressing him in a fresh toga, the three children carried their father downstairs to the atrium. They placed him on a table with his feet pointed towards the door, as was the custom. Timon said he would make an official announcement that afternoon, and invite Aquila's friends, colleagues, clients and freedmen to come and pay their respects.

Before they left, Val left careful instructions with Theodora on how to care for Simio. Then she hugged him close.

'See you very soon, Simmy,' she said to the chimpanzee. 'I'll send for you as soon as we're settled. You'll love it on the Palatine, I know you will.'

Lucius held his father's hand one last time. The flesh was cold and stiff now. He took off Aquila's chalcedony ring – he knew his father would want him to have it – and placed it on his own finger. From the altar of the household gods, in a niche in the atrium wall, he took the little wooden dog statue – his father's favourite. With these objects he would remember him. Then he gave a farewell hug to Argos.

'Carius,' he called to the freedman he trusted most, 'please look after my dog while I'm gone.'

'I will, sir,' said Carius, leading Argos away.

Soon afterwards, Lucius departed the house with Ennius, Quin and Valeria.

Eyeing Quin's bandaged feet, Ennius asked if he'd prefer to travel by litter. Quin waved the suggestion away. 'The injury is to my upper feet and toes,' he said. 'I can walk just fine.'

They wound their way down the steep path of the Esquiline, past the Flavian Amphitheatre, the great gilded statue of Sol the sun god, and the Temple of Venus and Rome, before joining the Via Sacra – the Sacred Way, Rome's most magnificent street.

Ennius tried to make conversation. 'You see there,' he said, pointing to a construction site just in front of the Forum. 'That's going to be the Arch of Titus, celebrating his victory in the Siege of Jerusalem. It's so sad that he never lived to see it completed. By the way, they say that Domitian's first act as emperor was to make his brother a god.'

Ennius eyed his companions. From their sombre expressions he concluded that a different topic of conversation was required. 'Do you have any idea who killed your father?' he asked.

Quin grunted. 'Can you talk about something else, friend – or, even better, say nothing at all!'

Ennius flinched at this outburst, and Lucius placed a calming hand on Quin's shoulder. 'We have no idea,' he replied to Ennius.

'Well, I hope the prefect catches him soon,' said Ennius. 'As I said, you're all in terrible danger. But you'll be able to relax very soon, once you're safely inside my master's residence.'

We're not there yet, though, thought Lucius, casting a wary eye on everyone they passed.

They headed up a gently curving road that led towards the summit of the Palatine Hill. This whole area had once formed part of the emperor Nero's extravagant palace, the Golden House. The builders had levelled a large section of the hillside to create a porticoed terrace. These days, it housed a row of expensive boutiques, selling religious artefacts, furnishings, rare spices and perfumes to the wealthy ladies who lived on the Palatine. But there was no trade today – the shops were all closed, their display windows shuttered, as a mark of respect for the passing of Titus. The only open door belonged to the last shop in the terrace. It stood ajar, revealing a dark interior. This struck Lucius as odd – but by then it was already too late...

As they passed the shop, half a dozen soldiers suddenly ran out, their swords raised. They carried the oval shields with moon-and-stars insignia of the Praetorians – the emperor's elite force of bodyguards. Before Lucius could react, the guards had grabbed all four of them and dragged them in through the shop doorway. The door closed, and Lucius felt himself being hurled violently into a wall. Pain shot through his back as he hit a set of shelves, sending clay jars raining down to shatter on the floor around his feet.

He heard Valeria screaming for help. In the dim light coming through the curtained window, he glimpsed Ennius wrestling free of his captor and making for the door. One of the soldiers cut him down before he got there, then ran him through with his sword. Ennius gurgled and fell still. Valeria's screams continued to echo around the small room, and when her captor clamped his hand over her mouth, she bit him, making him curse and strike her hard across the face.

Lucius was vaguely aware of a struggle going on between Quin and one of the soldiers on the far side of the room. Then he felt a sword tip pressed against his throat, and a sweat-beaded face beneath a crested helmet loomed very close. 'Prepare to die, son of a traitor,' the guardsman growled.

'What are you talking about?' grunted Lucius. 'What have we done?'

'We're wiping you out, you and your wretched family. You're a stain on Rome, all of you. Now get down on your knees.'

A powerful hand pushed his head down until his cheek was pressed against the cold stone floor.

He heard the whump of an iron-soled caliga* hitting a body, followed by another scream from Valeria. From the far side of the room came Quin's muffled voice. 'You'll have Consul Glabrio to answer to for this, murderers!'

This elicited laughter from the guards. There was a smacking sound and Quin groaned in pain.

'Executioners, you mean,' said a smooth, deep voice. A door at the back of the shop creaked open and the room was partially illuminated by a lantern glow. Lucius raised his eyes to see who had just come in. The man was unhelmeted, but otherwise wore the same uniform as the others – though from his gleaming bronze chestplate and silver-handled gladius,** he looked senior.

'I am Aulus Galerius Scaro,' he announced,

* caliga: army boot.
** gladius: infantry sword.

'Tribune of the Third Praetorian Cohort.* My men are not thugs. They do not commit murder.' His eyes narrowed to slits as he dropped to his haunches and looked intently at Lucius. 'You'll be beheaded, as befits your patrician** status, even though you don't deserve it, you spawn of a snake.'

'Hold still,' barked Lucius's captor. The hand took a firmer grip on Lucius's head. Lucius closed his eyes tight, anticipating the end.

I'll be with you soon, Father!

'Wait,' snapped Scaro. 'I didn't tell you to kill them yet, did I? First I want to find out what they know, and what they've told others – like the city prefect, for example.' The tribune leaned close to Lucius. 'What did your father tell you?'

His fingers, sliding through the dust of the floor, encountered the edge of a shard from one of the broken clay jars. He could feel its sharpness. If he could only grab hold of it…

'Speak!' shouted Scaro impatiently.

'He told us nothing!' Lucius croaked.

'I would advise you to tell the truth,' said Scaro mildly, 'or else Fulvianus here will make your death extremely slow and painful. What did your father say to you?'

Lucius felt the jab of a sword tip near the top of his spine.

---

* *tribune: commander; cohort: army unit.*
** *patrician: aristocratic.*

'I'm not telling you anything,' Lucius rasped, as he reached desperately for the shard.

The sword bit deeper into the flesh of Lucius's back, making him yell out in pain.

'What did he say to you?' asked Scaro again.

'That Titus was murdered,' said Quin fiercely. 'He was going to make a speech in the Senate about it today – but you lot killed him.'

Scaro laughed. 'The Divine Titus was not murdered. He died of a fever. Your father was acting out of pure malice. It was a pathetic attempt to undermine the legitimacy of the new emperor... Oh, and by the way, we had nothing to do with Aquila's death – though I can't say I shed many tears when I heard about it. Now tell me, have you passed on his treasonous falsehood to anyone else?'

'We spoke to no one,' said Quin.

'Tell the truth!' Scaro suddenly roared. 'Or watch your sister die in pain!' He dragged Valeria to her feet and held a sword to her neck.

By stretching his arm almost out of its socket, Lucius managed to pinch the clay shard between two fingertips and then slowly drag it into his hand. It was long and sharp like a dagger blade. He counted six guardsmen in the room, as well as Scaro. They had no chance of beating them – but he, at least, would go down fighting...

He tried to catch Quin's eye to warn him of what he was about to do, but his brother could only stare, dry-mouthed, at the sword next to Valeria's throat.

'Don't kill her – please,' groaned Quin.

Lucius knew he had to act quickly, before Scaro killed Val. With a sudden burst of energy, he pulled his head clear of Fulvianus's hand and whirled around, plunging the tip of the shard as hard as he could into the guardsman's unprotected thigh. Fulvianus screamed, and Lucius felt warm blood pour onto his fingers. Quin, with his lightning reflexes, reacted half a second quicker than anyone else in the room, breaking free of his own captor and pushing Scaro away from Valeria. But before the three of them could make it to the door, guardsmen quickly surrounded them.

Lucius knew their only chance lay in single-mindedly attack. The shop interior was small and dark, hampering the movement and vision of the soldiers. Also, their swords were long and required space to be swung freely. Lucius leapt at one of the men who was blocking their way. He grabbed the man's head and drove a knee into his stomach. The soldier groaned and fell backwards to the ground, but managed to pull Lucius with him in a tight bearhug. Quin was a blur of movement to his left, seeming to take on two soldiers with nothing but his fists. To his right, Valeria was punching and kicking like a wildcat.

In the steely grip of the soldier, Lucius felt the air being squeezed out of his chest. He couldn't breathe, let alone move. He heard scuffles and muffled cries, and it didn't sound good for either his brother or sister.

Their resistance had lasted all of five seconds.

'Bring them here,' ordered a furious-sounding Scaro. 'Make them kneel before me. I want to see their heads roll.'

Air flowed back into Lucius's lungs as he felt himself being lifted clear of the ground. Fulvianus was clutching a blood-soaked rag to his thigh. His red-rimmed eyes glared murderously at Lucius. 'Let me deal with that one, sir,' he snarled.

'Be my guest,' said Scaro.

Once again, Lucius found himself forced to his knees with his head pushed hard against the ground. He could hear Fulvianus's grunting breaths and smell his blood and sweat.

And then a shadow darkened the floor, and the room suddenly echoed to a wild shriek. There was a whoosh and a thump. Fulvianus screamed once again and fell backwards. Lucius looked up in time to see something dark with shining teeth clamped to the guardsman's neck.

CHAPTER IV

15 SEPTEMBER

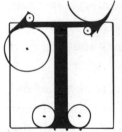he man holding Valeria started backwards in fright when he saw the thing biting Fulvianus. In doing so, he knocked the lantern onto his colleague, whose cloak caught alight. In the panic that followed, Lucius grabbed Valeria's hand and pulled her to her feet. Quin fought off his own captor, and the three of them raced for the door. As soon as they were out on the street, Lucius felt Valeria tugging him back again. 'We can't leave yet!' she cried.

'Why?'

'Simio's still in there.'

Lucius stared. 'That grinning demon was Simio?'

Val nodded. 'He saved our lives.'

There was another bloodcurdling shriek before the chimpanzee pushed aside the curtain covering the shop window and jumped out to join them. Smoke was by now pouring from the shop, as one of the guardsmen staggered, retching, through the door.

'This way!' yelled Quin, leading them up the long curve of the hill. 'We have to get to Glabrio's – it's the only safe place.'

But before they'd covered ten yards, they were confronted by a devastating sight: a troop of about thirty Praetorians were marching at full tilt down the hill towards them. They spun around and began running back the way they had come, but their original abductors had by now emerged from the shop, coughing and spluttering. Scaro looked mad with rage. 'Get after them!' he cried.

With soldiers closing in on both sides, they appeared trapped, but Simio, being a chimp, didn't think twice about what to do next. He immediately ran to the edge of the road and took a flying leap off the side of the hill. Hearts in mouths, Lucius, Val and Quin ran to the place where he had jumped and saw that he'd landed on the tiled roof of a temple just ten feet below. With soldiers now closing in behind them, they had no choice but to follow his lead.

They jumped.

Pain blazed in Lucius's knees and ankles as he landed awkwardly on the sloping roof. He tried to grab hold of something to stop himself falling further, but the momentum of the jump sent him rolling down the roof. Just as he was about to tumble right over the edge, he flung out an arm and caught hold of a gilded statue of the winged goddess Victory. He dangled there for a moment, clinging on with his fingers, until with a sickening crumbling sound the statue toppled. Lucius squeezed his eyes closed and braced himself.

He landed sooner than he had expected, with a jarring thud to his right shoulder. Lightning forks of pain radiated from that region through every bone. He smelled and tasted blood and ash. He was lying on a massive block of carved marble – an altar, its surface black from centuries of burnt offerings. For a moment, he could only lie there, blinking slowly. Then warm, strong hands helped him off the slab to the ground.

'We can't stay here,' murmured Quin. 'Can you walk?'

They were standing in the shadow of a row of thick columns at the top of a long set of steps.

One of Lucius's ankles felt tender. He put weight on it and found he could bear the pain. 'I think so. Where's Val?'

'She fell down on the other side of the temple. Let's go.'

Rubbing his sore shoulder, Lucius limped after Quin as he skirted the temple's pillared exterior. Was his brother a cat? How had he landed so painlessly? On the western side of the building was an ancient-looking grove. Val and Simio had enjoyed a softer landing – caught by the branches of a small dogwood tree growing close to the roof. Simio hooted with excitement when he saw Quin and Lucius, and clambered down to greet them. Val edged her way down the trunk a little more hesitantly. When Lucius saw the big red bruise on her cheek where a Praetorian had struck her, his jaw clenched with anger. They hugged briefly. Then he patted Simio on the head. 'I knew I had made the right decision, taking you into our family,' he said.

'I told you Simmy always knows when we're in danger,' said Val proudly. 'He must have escaped from the house and come straight to us.' She hugged the chimp. 'Didn't you, you clever, clever boy?'

'Hoo-hoo. Ah-ah-ah!' cried Simio approvingly.

'His timing couldn't have been better,' admitted Quin, 'but we're not out of danger yet. Those Praetorians will be all over this place in the next few minutes.'

'Where can we go?' wondered Lucius. 'I can't see how we can get to Glabrio's house now.'

Quin cast a rueful glance back up the hill. 'Yeah, I'm afraid that's out of the question. It's where they're expecting us to go.'

They looked around them. Below, the crowds were moving along the Via Sacra, heading to and from the Forum. Many were wearing a dark grey or brown toga pulla, the garment worn during periods of mourning. Lucius pondered the idea of simply losing themselves in the great throng, but quickly dismissed it – the Praetorians were everywhere; it would only be a matter of time before they were spotted.

'What about going back home?' suggested Val.

'Sorry, sis,' said Quin. 'We can't go anywhere expected. There are ten thousand Praetorian guards in this city. Basically, nowhere's safe.' He looked at them grimly. 'We've got no choice. We have to get out of Rome.'

'How?' Lucius asked.

Quin began walking through the grove. 'Follow me,' he called. 'I've got an idea.' Lucius and Valeria, with Simio bounding along beside them, followed.

'What's happened, Lu?' asked Val as they went. 'Why are all the Praetorians suddenly trying to kill us? And why can't Glabrio stop them?'

'I wish I knew,' grimaced Lucius, trying to ignore the pain shooting from various parts of his body. 'As I understand it, the Praetorians are totally loyal to the emperor, which means that it's probably him who wants to kill us – and he's got all the power. Glabrio may be consul but that doesn't mean a thing. If Domitian wants us dead, there's nothing Glabrio or anyone else can do about it.'

'Why does Domitian want us dead? Doesn't he want people to know his brother was murdered?'

Lucius glanced at her, shaking his head in wonder at her innocence. 'Not if he was the one who ordered his murder.'

Val paled when she heard this, and bit her lip. 'I so wish Father was alive,' she murmured.

They emerged from the grove by the wall of the House of the Vestals, priestesses of the goddess Vesta. From here, Quin led them south along the Nova Via – once a famous road, now disused and choked with weeds. They passed the ruins of the Palace of Tiberius, which had been gutted during the fire the previous year. Luckily, this part of the hill was devoid of people, but they still had to be careful. They followed Quin's lead, moving in darting little runs between the fallen pillars and crumbling walls, overgrown with brittle, sun-browned bushes and creepers.

At length, they reached a low stone wall, beyond which lay the proscenium of the temple of Cybele, the Great Mother. This was a wide, flat space of white stone, dominated by an altar, which served as a stage for festivities in honour of the goddess. To the left was a long flight of steps, above which towered the marble columns of Cybele's temple. Quin hastily dropped to a crouch, dipping his head below the top of the wall, and indicated for the others to do the same. On the far side of the proscenium a troop of Praetorians stood on watch.

'We have to get past them somehow,' whispered Quin.

'Why?' asked Lucius.

'Because it's our only chance of getting out of this city,' replied Quin cryptically.

Lucius quickly saw that there was no route they

could take that would keep them out of sight of the guards – this part of the hill was simply too exposed. Then he noticed some activity going on above them. A line of priests, dressed in hooded robes, were processing slowly down the temple steps, chanting and clashing cymbals as they went. He pointed them out to Quin, who immediately understood his brother's plan.

Beckoning to Val and Simio to follow, they crept some fifty paces eastwards, further up the hill, taking care to keep out of sight below the wall, until they arrived at another set of steps leading to the north side of the temple. They were now out of sight of the Praetorians. Quin raised his finger to his lips. It was a sign even Simio understood, and the chimp was as quiet as the rest of them as they ascended the steps. When they reached the top, they turned right and ran swiftly along the shaded portico surrounding the temple, until they came to the western side, which overlooked the proscenium. Taking cover behind a pillar, they watched the priests continue to file out of the temple through an arched entrance.

As the last of the robed figures emerged, Quin and Lucius signalled to each other, then leapt out together. Lucius grabbed hold of one of the priests and wrestled him to the floor, clamping a hand to his mouth before he could cry out. Meanwhile, Quin yanked another pair of priests by their hoods into the temple interior. Lucius joined him there with his own captive, followed soon after by Val and Simio. The priests gazed at their captors with terrified eyes as Quin gestured to them to be quiet, drawing his finger across his throat as a warning. They didn't move or say a word as they were hastily stripped of their robes. The only protest seemed to come from the giant enthroned statue of Cybele, who glared sternly at the interlopers from the rear of the cella.* Lucius silently vowed to make an offering to the Great Mother, as soon as he got the chance, to atone for this offence against her. Then he and Quin bound the priests with a set of large golden collars more usually employed for putting around the necks of sacrificial bulls.

A minute later, three priestly figures emerged from the temple and hastened down the steps to join the end of the procession. The third of these latecomers had a somewhat strange shape, being quite small in height, yet surprisingly wide. This was Valeria, who was attempting to descend the steps while sharing her robe with Simio. Lucius, in front of her, had a nightmarish vision of girl and chimp tripping on the hem of the too-large robe and falling forwards, sending him, Quin and the entire line of priests tumbling to an undignified death at the bottom of the steps.

Luckily, they made it down to the proscenium without incident. From here the priests began to circumnavigate the wide rectangular space. Lucius could see that a white bullock with gilded horns was being led by one of the foremost priests, and that the

---

* cella: the inner chamber of a temple, housing a statue of the god or goddess.

circuitous procession would eventually lead to the altar. Before they got there, though, they would have to pass very close to the Praetorians.

Quin glanced back at him and murmured: 'Be ready to follow me.'

The pace of the procession was painfully slow and Lucius's skin itched from the rough fabric of the robe. They had reached the southwestern corner of the proscenium, and were getting very close to the Praetorians, when Simio started getting nervous.

'Ooh-ooh! Ah-ah-ah!' he panted.

Lucius glanced behind him in alarm. He could see that some sort of struggle was taking place under Val's robe, which was shaking and bulging in different directions.

'O! O! O! O!' cried the strange-looking priest. 'Huuuu! O! O! O!'

The priest in front of Quin turned his head and frowned. 'What is going on back there?' he demanded.

'The goddess has possessed him,' explained Quin from beneath his hood. 'Our brother is in a state of… rapture.'

'Cybele be praised,' added Lucius.

At this point, a small furry hand slipped out from beneath Val's robe, before quickly being pulled out of sight.

'What was that?' gasped the startled priest.

'Nothing!' smiled Lucius.

'I definitely saw something hairy!'

Lucius had to think fast. He remembered that Cybele, the Great Mother, was sometimes linked with nature and wild animals. 'He's been praying very hard lately,' he stammered. 'He may have turned a little, um, wild…'

'Well, just make sure he stays quiet and keeps himself covered until the ceremony is over,' ordered the priest, with a final nervous glance at the strange one. 'I shall be reporting this incident to the chief priest.'

As soon as the man had returned his gaze to the front, Quin began to veer off to the right. Lucius and Val (still struggling with Simio) followed him to the edge of the proscenium. Before anyone noticed, they stepped onto a steep, narrow path that led down the hill. They had to pass within a few yards of the Praetorians, and Lucius prayed they wouldn't be seen.

'Ooh-ooh-ooh! Owww!' cried Simio.

One of the Praetorians glanced towards them, but his view was partially blocked by bushes.

'Keep him quiet!' hissed Quin.

'Mmmmmffff,' said the chimp, as a hand was clamped firmly over his mouth.

'Sorry Simmy,' whispered Val.

The guard looked away.

With a sigh of relief, Val allowed the agitated chimp to escape, and he went bounding off along the path. The three of them, after discarding their robes, followed him. A hundred paces further along, the trees to their right parted and a spectacular view opened up.

'The Circus Maximus!' cried Lucius. 'Is that where you're taking us, brother? Are you expecting us to escape from Rome in a racing chariot?'

To his surprise, Quin merely smiled and nodded.

'You're joking, right?'

But Quin was already running down the hillside towards the giant oval stadium.

The closer they got, the thicker the crowds grew. Hundreds of racegoers were gathered on the Palatine's lower slopes and around the stadium entrances. Lucius kept his eyes alert for the gleam of Praetorian armour, but saw none. The stadium doors were closed, and by the disgruntled expressions on the faces of many, there didn't seem any prospect of them opening.

They picked their way through the dense press of bodies to the western end of the Circus Maximus, known as the officium. It consisted of a long, slightly convex wall of twelve high arches through which horses, chariots and riders entered and left the stadium. The arches led directly to the carceres, or starting gates, from which the races began. The open area in front of the officium was fenced off to the public. The stadium official manning the gate was looking flustered after a morning spent fielding complaints from the disappointed crowd. However, Quin was well known to him and the man waved him and his siblings through. It was fortunate that, with all the commotion, he failed to notice the chimpanzee lolloping casually alongside Val.

The concourse outside the stadium was also bustling with activity. There were horses, grooms, stable-boys, trainers, charioteers, harnessmen, doctors and clerks from each of the four teams, all identifiable from the colour of their belts or tunics. There were also a few troopers from the city battalions, but luckily no Praetorians.

Quin risked approaching one of the White team's grooms. 'Hey, Pertinax,' he called out, 'what's going on?'

The groom, who was emerging from one of the arched entrances, looked up. He grinned when he recognised Quin.

'No racing today,' he said. 'The Roman Games are cancelled because of the emperor's death. Everyone's very upset – but then you know what race fans are like. The sky might fall and the Tiber might run dry, but the races must go on!'

Quin laughed heartily, turning on the charm. 'Hey, Pertinax,' he said, 'is there any chance I could borrow a quadriga* and four of your best stallions?'

The groom frowned. 'What do you want them for? We're taking them all back to the stables now on the Campus Martius.'**

'It's my brother's birthday,' he said, pointing at Lucius. 'I wanted to give him a special treat. Take him

---

* *quadriga: a chariot drawn by four horses abreast.*
** *Campus Martius: an area outside the city walls which had many fine public buildings.*

for a quick ride down the Via Appia*... Just a mile or so. Tell you what, I'll deliver the chariot and horses back to the stables myself later. Save you a journey.'

'Well, it's not really allowed, Quintus. You know the rules. These chariots are built for the track, not the open road.'

Quin raised his eyebrows and opened his arms in a gesture of humble entreaty. 'Would you deny me this one little favour, Pertinax, after my performance three days ago – finishing a race even after being sabotaged?'

'This could cost me my job, Quintus,' said Pertinax, clearly distressed by what he was being asked to do.

Quin took him aside and whispered something in his ear. As he spoke, the groom began to look more closely at Lucius and his expression changed from one of fear to pity. Pertinax thought for a moment, then beckoned them to follow him back inside the officium.

'What did you just say to him?' Lucius wanted to know.

'Told him you were dying,' Quin murmured. 'Told him this was your final wish. So look sick, will you?'

While Lucius did his best to appear weak, Pertinax led them to a row of stalls set into a corner of the building. Four sleek, black, muscular horses were there, feeding from their hay baskets. 'These are among the very best,' said Pertinax, '– all raised on top North African stud farms.'

* Via Appia (or Appian Way). the main road from Rome to Brundisium (modern Brindisi) in the south of Italy.

'Of course, I've raced with them,' said Quin, going to each in turn and giving it an affectionate pat on the forelock. 'Ferox, Icarus, Cupido and, wait, don't tell me… Polydoxes. Thank you, Pertinax.'

The groom began harnessing the horses to one of the chariots. A long shaft extended from the front of the vehicle. Near the tip of the shaft was a crossbar to which the two inner horses were yoked. The outer horses were linked to the inner ones with sturdy ropes. To Lucius, the chariot looked like little more than a basket on wheels, with a curved latticework front and a small platform to stand on above the axle. 'Are you serious?' he muttered to Quin. 'Three of us, plus an overgrown monkey, on that?'

'It'll be fine,' Quin assured him.

When the chariot was ready, Quin stepped aboard and took up the reins. He made a soft clicking sound with his tongue and the horses started forward. Pertinax, Lucius and Val, with Simio holding her hand, followed the chariot out of the officium.

'I'll see you back at the stables, then?' said Pertinax, with a quick nervous glance over his shoulder in case one of the team managers or trainers was watching.

'Have no fear,' said Quin.

'I hope you enjoy the trip,' Pertinax said to Lucius. 'I'm sorry to hear about your – uh – condition.'

Val looked puzzled. 'What condition?' she started to say, but Lucius interrupted with a forced coughing fit. He was about to thank Pertinax when he glimpsed a blood-chilling sight just beyond the groom's head: at least fifty white-crested helmets were bobbing towards them at high speed – Praetorian cavalry arriving from the north along the Vicus Tuscus.*

Quin saw them, too. 'Quick, get on board,' he yelled, and Lucius and Val squeezed themselves onto the chariot's small platform. Simio levered himself up onto the wicker frame before leaping onto the shaft between the horses. Balancing on the narrow beam, the chimp stood up and placed a hand on the hindquarters of each of the inner horses. He looked ahead, almost as if he imagined himself to be the driver.

'Oo-Oo-Ooh!' he hooted excitedly.

Quin needed no further encouragement. With a flick of the reins, they took off.

The surge of power took Lucius completely by surprise and he felt himself losing balance and toppling off the back. At the last moment, Val, who was clinging onto the chariot's frame with one hand, managed to grab him with the other and haul him back on board. He barely had time to draw breath before the air was split by a loud crack and the four of them were hurled several feet into the air. They collapsed back into the chariot, which was now teetering from side to side, seemingly out of control. Somehow, Quin managed to keep it upright and on course. Glancing behind, Lucius saw the wreckage of a section of the concourse fencing,

* *Vicus Tuscus: a street that ran from the Circus Maximus to the Forum Romanum.*

which they'd just smashed through. Beyond that stood a seriously alarmed Pertinax. Lucius watched the lead Praetorian cavalry officer pull up by the frightened groom and start to cross-examine him.

'We're doomed!' shouted Lucius above the clatter of hooves. 'Pertinax will tell them it was us, then they'll chase us down.'

'I can easily outstrip them with these four beauties,' promised Quin. 'They're built for the sprint.'

Lucius was comforted by his brother's calm confidence – and he could almost believe they had a chance as he watched the four handsome black horses, their manes billowing in the wind, charging seemingly without effort along the wide, smooth road. They were overtaking the carts and foot traffic almost as if these were standing still. But what would happen when the horses tired? The races at the Circus Maximus were just over three miles long, and that was the distance these horses were accustomed to. That might take them a little way beyond the gates of the city, but no further.

Perhaps it's best not to think about that now.

Lucius had been living from second to second, crisis to crisis, from the moment he'd woken up this morning. There had been no time to assess what had happened to them or to plan ahead. It was a way of living that seemed to come more easily to his brother and sister than to him. While they were taking it all in their stride, it made him feel giddy, out of control.

But he had to admit there was something exciting about it, too. For one thing, he'd never travelled this fast before – he liked the way the wind pummelled his face and whipped at his hair, and it gave him a hint of the exhilaration Quin must experience when racing in the Circus Maximus.

They were on the Via Appia, heading southeast through the city suburbs. To their left was the Caelian Hill, where the pink roofs of grand villas could be seen poking up between the dark green canopy of cypresses and pines. On their right were the eastern foothills of the Aventine Hill, out of which snaked an immensely tall aqueduct, supported on three tiers of arches.

Ahead of them loomed the impressive brown-stone barricade of the Servian Wall, marking the edge of the city. The gates of Porta Capena stood permanently open – it had been decades since the city had bothered to maintain guards on the wall, and centuries since it had actually needed them.

On the far side of the gates they saw, to the south, the glittering blue expanse of the Piscina Publica, an enormous reservoir and public swimming pool. Shortly after that, the road entered a cutting, with steep grassy banks to either side. When they emerged, the view opened up to encompass woods, meadows and the private estates of the rich, extending to a distant horizon of hills and mountains. There was no sign of a chasing column of Praetorian cavalry to the rear, and Lucius tried to relax.

'Pertinax must have been braver than you gave him credit for,' said Quin. 'We Whites are loyal to each other – and everyone hates the Praetorians.'

'You think he lied to them?' asked Lucius.

Quin nodded. 'He probably said I was Lepontus, that scoundrel from the Reds who wrecked my chariot in the last race.'

The thought made Lucius smile.

The road was beautifully smooth – its surface made up of tight-fitting interlocking stones that had been worn to a glassy sheen after centuries of use. The horses seemed almost to glide along.

'This is one of the earliest roads our people built,' Lucius remarked. 'Nearly four hundred years old.'

'Father told you that, right?' said Val.

Lucius nodded, and a lump formed in his throat, preventing him from saying any more. He felt Val's hand on his arm, and he appreciated her attempt to comfort him.

'You were the closest to him, Lu,' she said. 'He loved you the best.'

Lucius shook his head. 'Not true.' But inside he felt once again his father's warm hands on his shoulders and that connection, deep beyond words. Instinctively, he rubbed the chalcedony ring.

He remembered something else his father had once told him about the Via Appia – something too gruesome to share with Val, but it resonated with his current mood. Just over 150 years ago, Spartacus the gladiator and his army of slaves had rebelled against the Romans. They held out for two years, winning many battles, but were eventually defeated by the Roman general Marcus Licinius Crassus. Six thousand slaves were captured, and Crassus ordered the crucifixion of every one of them along this very road. The crosses stretched 120 miles along the Via Appia, from Rome to Capua. Lucius could almost imagine the shadows of those crosses falling upon the road, just like the shadow of Fulvianus's sword that had lain across his neck this morning. They had not yet escaped that shadow, and the thought made his stomach tighten with fear.

They stopped that evening at the settlement of Forum Appii, forty-three miles southeast of Rome. By this time the horses, built for sprinting, were exhausted and barely able to go faster than a trot. As they arrived, they were immediately approached by stable owners and innkeepers offering their services. The three travellers looked at each other. They hadn't even thought about money. Val had brought nothing. Lucius and Quin quickly checked their money pouches. They had about three hundred denarii between them – enough for a few days on the road. Quin went off to stable the horses, and bribed the stable-boy to provide a separate stall for Simio. Meanwhile, Lucius and Val rented a room at an inn across the street.

As the three of them ate their evening meal of leeks in vinegar and boiled sheep's lips, Lucius posed the obvious question: 'So where shall we go?'

'I have a hankering to go down south, to see Calabria,' said Quin.

'That's where your friend Trebellius came from, right?' said Lucius.

Quin nodded sadly. 'He said it's beautiful country.'

Trebellius had been a fellow gladiator at the Ludus Romanus whom Quin had been forced to kill in the arena. He'd never got over the guilt, and this was the reason he'd stopped being a gladiator.

'What'll we do for money?' wondered Lucius.

'We'll manage,' said Quin, winking at Valeria. 'We did it before, didn't we?'

'I can work as a fuller,' said Val, remembering her time laundering gladiator outfits.

'That's the spirit,' smiled Quin. He put down his fork and took the hands of his brother and sister. 'We'll get through this,' he vowed to them. 'The three of us, together forever, right? We'll make Father proud.'

CHAPTER V

16 SEPTEMBER

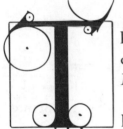hey left early the next morning, continuing south through the Pontine Marshes, heading towards Tarracina.*

'Pooh!' commented Val, wrinkling her nose. 'Stinks around here.'

The road had been built on a stone causeway that raised it above the marshland. All that could be seen for miles in either direction was a flat, misty landscape of grass, reeds and foul-smelling stagnant pools.

'Lucius, do you remember our march through here on the way to Pompeii?' chuckled Quin.

'How could I forget?'

'The jokes about Crassus and his digestion!'

---

* Tarracina: a coastal town about 55 km southeast of Rome, now called Terracina.

They were perhaps ten miles along the nineteen-mile ruler-straight causeway when Lucius heard a sound behind them like distant thunder. He turned and saw a cloud of yellow dust on the horizon. For some reason he thought again of the shadow of Fulvianus's sword, and a chill settled on his heart.

'Speed up, brother,' he said. 'Let's not spend any longer than we have to in this wretched place.'

Quin flashed a smile and flicked the reins.

Five minutes later, the dust cloud was a lot closer, and Val and Quin had noticed it, too. Mounted figures were visible within the cloud, and a sound of hundreds of hoofbeats shook the air.

'Are they…?' Val left the question hanging, not daring to complete it.

Lucius could only stare at what was coming.

Quin's face had turned hard and dark, almost like bronze. He whipped at the horses' flanks, exhorting them to go faster.

'The innkeeper must have told them about us,' muttered Lucius bitterly. 'He took our money, and then he took theirs.'

'They might not be Praetorians,' said Val desperately – though by now there was no mistaking the white crests and the gleam of armour. 'Or they may be after someone else.'

'This is the worst place to get caught,' said Quin, grinding his jaw in frustration. 'Nothing but marshes for miles – no place to hide.'

Val clung tightly to Lucius as the cavalry drew ever closer. Soon it was possible to see the cold, piercing expressions of the officers at the head of the column. The entire causeway trembled under the pounding of hooves. However hard and often Quin lashed at his horses, he and the others knew it was hopeless. The horses' mouths were now white with saliva – they were tiring.

'Together forever,' Quin reminded them. 'Say it!'

'Together forever!' Val and Lucius chorused.

Within minutes, an outrider had raced ahead of the main cavalry force and drawn alongside the chariot. Val screamed and Lucius cowered as the Praetorian raised his spear, readying himself to fling it at them. At that moment, Simio sprang up from his seat on the chariot shaft and grabbed hold of the neck of the cavalryman's horse. This so startled the horse that it began to whinny and buck. Simio somehow clung on, his legs swinging wildly through the air. The cavalryman unleashed his spear, but it missed its aim, striking the chariot's wheel. There was a wrenching, clattering screech as the spear got caught in the spokes. Val cannoned into Lucius, who smashed into Quin, who very nearly fell out of the chariot. All three were then thrown violently to the right as the wheel on that side splintered and collapsed. For a few terrifying seconds, Lucius found himself flat on his stomach, nose just a hand's breadth from the road, watching the axle strike sparks on the flat stone surface.

Then the chariot must have flipped right over, because he was flying and bouncing and rolling at bruising, dizzying speed across the road. He came to rest, finally, in a heap by the side of the road. Below him was the edge of the causeway: a short cliff of piled stones plunging into a thick, brown, bubbling pool. His knees and elbows felt raw and sticky with blood. His ankle screamed with pain.

Something soft brushed against his fingers. Twisting his head around, he saw Val lying there beside him, brown with dust, a bloody scrape on her arm. She was trying to clasp his hand. Behind her, Praetorians were dismounting from their horses, unsheathing their swords, and running towards them.

Lucius rose to his knees, ignoring the piercing pain in his ankle, and attempted to cover Val with his body, wanting to protect her for as long as possible from the stabbing blades. She looked up at him and managed a smile. 'Together forever,' she breathed.

From behind them came an animal roar. Lucius looked back and saw Quin, tunic ripped, covered in blood, rising to his feet and charging towards the oncoming soldiers. This was accompanied by wild chimpanzee shrieks and violent shaking of the branches of a small myrtle tree on the far side of the road.

'Run!' Quin yelled at Lucius and Val as he charged. 'Run for your lives!' He turned to face the Praetorians, widening his arms as he went. The Praetorians closed on Quin in disciplined ranks, six abreast.

'No!!!' screamed Val as she saw Quin collide with them. The first three soldiers were knocked backwards by the force of his impact, but others quickly surrounded and engulfed him.

'No!' she cried again as their brother disappeared from view. She kept repeating the word while Lucius, sobbing, tried to drag her down the ledge of stones. Quin was gone – dead. But he needn't have died in vain. Maybe Lucius and Val could still escape if they moved quickly, taking advantage of the distraction Quin had caused by his self-sacrifice. With his injured ankle, Lucius knew he couldn't run, but perhaps they could hide down there in the stinking mud, and pray that the Praetorians wouldn't follow.

But to Lucius's dismay, Val slipped his grip and got to her feet. Crying hysterically, she staggered towards the place where Quin had fallen. Lucius could only watch as the Praetorians grabbed her and pinned her to the ground. He squeezed his eyes shut and bit back a scream of despair. Then he let his body slide over the precipice.

He fell with barely a splash into the warm, fetid soup. It was not so different from the tepidarium* at the Baths of Titus, except for the sticky thickness of the water, which enveloped him like a liquid cloak. He didn't try to swim. Instead, he sank to the soft, mushy, slippery bottom and waited there. Did he have the courage to kill himself? If he opened his mouth now

* tepidarium: the warm room in a Roman bath.

and drank, it would all be over very quickly. Surely that was the best option, with his father, brother and sister all dead. All that awaited him if he tried to grab a breath up there would be a spear in the throat. Better, surely, to stay down here and surrender himself to Antheia, goddess of swamps.

There was a splash nearby, then another. He opened his eyes a fraction and caught a dim glint of long, sharp objects falling around him, plunging into the muddy bed. They were throwing their spears down here, trying to finish him off. It was time, surely, to open his mouth and welcome death.

But Lucius's muscles rebelled. His body still wanted life, even if his mind didn't. Without willing it, he began to crawl along the muddy, reedy bottom, pushing forward with his arms and his good leg. His lungs cried for air – they were like a pair of clenched fists inside his chest, getting steadily tighter. But he couldn't rise to the surface – not yet! – the soldiers would see him. He could hear the muffled sobs of his throat as he frantically pulled himself forward. His heart was hammering at him like an enemy, making him dizzy. He was desperate to open his mouth and let it all be over, but his lips refused to part. Lucius knew he was growing weaker. His limbs had become jelly, but still he pushed on.

He was seeing lights behind his eyelids, and Lucius guessed this must be the approach of death. Yet it didn't seem like death. Sounds were becoming sharper

– sounds of wind in grass and the buzz of insects. He felt warm sun on his shoulders. The water had become shallow. He flopped onto his side and opened his mouth. His chest heaved, air whistled into his throat. He coughed and retched. The air smelled foul, like the breath of Hades – but it was air. His breathing became steadier.

When his strength had returned, he opened his mud-encrusted eyes and took in the scene. He was lying in a shallow, swampy area, thick with reeds. Through gaps in the reeds he glimpsed the causeway about twenty paces away. Praetorians were gathered at its edge, peering into the water, lances poised like spear fishermen. A few were scanning the marshes, sometimes looking in his direction, but they couldn't see him, caked as he was in thick, gooey mud and half hidden by reeds. Behind the soldiers he could see the body of his brother draped over a horse. His sister was seated behind the saddle of another horse, her wrists bound. So she hadn't been killed! A groan of relief escaped his lips. They must have decided she posed no threat. Or – and his blood turned to ice at the thought – they were planning to torture her as a way of forcing him to reveal himself.

But the Praetorians didn't touch her. Instead, they continued to search the marshes, a couple of them even getting in and wading in the area where Lucius had dived, poking at the muddy bottom with their spears.

There was no sign of the horses from the Circus

Maximus. They must have charged off in fear, dragging the wreckage of the chariot behind them. Nor could he see Simio anywhere about. The chimp had probably escaped across the marshes. Lucius hoped he would keep watch on his mistress from a safe distance – maybe even find some opportunity to rescue her.

The sun was well past its zenith by the time the Praetorians departed, seemingly satisfied that their quarry had drowned. Lucius continued lying there for a long time after they had gone, scarcely moving, ignoring the flies that buzzed around him. He'd got used to the smell, and felt strangely consoled by his muddy state. He'd lost half his family, and been forced to flee the city. He felt stripped of his Romanness, his humanity even. It seemed right somehow that he should lie here like a dumb animal, unmoving, with scarcely a thought in his head.

Yet, as the hours went by, and thoughts and memories began to return, Lucius could no longer hold back the great tide of grief. Tears began to fall, making pale tracks in the mud on his cheeks – tears for his father, his brother, his sister, himself. Once they had started, he found they wouldn't stop. Even after his eyes had finally dried up, he continued to sob and shake. He wanted to die. He wished he could just close his eyes and never wake up.

Or did he?

He could have opened his mouth down there in the muddy deeps, let the marsh goddess take him. But he hadn't. Part of him, he realised, wanted to stay alive, if only to avenge his father and his brother, and to rescue Valeria. It seemed like a faint hope right now, in his current state. His damaged ankle, now resting in the muddy shallows, had become bluish-red and very swollen. The slightest pressure on it was agony. If he stayed here, he would die soon enough of exposure or thirst. But if he could somehow get back to the road, he could lay himself down there, and perhaps a well-meaning traveller might stop and pick him up. And then one day, when he'd regained his strength, he could go in search of the people who had destroyed his life, and kill them.

So, as the sun began to sink into the Tyrrhenian Sea, Lucius began the painful process of crawling and limping back towards the causeway. It took a long time, and he uttered a great many curses along the way, but, with a final wrenching effort, he hauled himself back up onto the road. Once there, he lay on his back as the light dimmed around him and the chill breeze turned the mud hard and grey on his skin.

'Wake up!' Lucius felt the whack of a hard leather sandal in his ribs. His eyes flew open. The sun dazzled, forcing him to squint. Above him loomed an immensely tall, bulky figure. Lucius felt himself being yanked roughly to his feet. He screamed as weight was placed on his ankle, then toppled back to the ground. His eyes closed again, trying to shut out a scary world. There followed a murmur of voices and he felt hands on him, pushing and prodding, but was too weak to protest.

The second time he was raised up, it was done more gently. He was hoisted onto the giant's shoulder, then laid on his back on a straw-covered wooden floor. A door clanged shut, and he found himself looking out through the bars of a small, iron-latticed cage. The cage swayed a little, and somewhere a horse snorted. He realised he was on a wagon – a caged wagon. Through the bars he could see the Pontine Marshes and the causeway, and the giant grinning at him. He had a gleaming bald head and a bronze band encircling one of his heavily muscled arms.

Another man joined him. This one was short and fat, with a small beard. He wore a brown cloak and a grubby linen head-covering. He gabbled some words in a foreign tongue to the giant, who grunted a reply. Then the fat man turned to Lucius and said in a loud, slow voice: 'Do you speak Latin?'

Lucius nodded.

'I am Abdosir. You belong to me now. I was returning from a profitable trip to the slave market in Rome when I saw you lying by the side of the road. At first I thought you were dead, and was most gratified to find that you were not. I have examined you and I think you will fetch a reasonable price back in my home country. The ankle will mend. What is your name, boy?'

Lucius didn't answer. He couldn't bring himself to say a name that no longer meant anything to him.

Abdosir grew impatient. 'Do you have a tongue in your head, boy? If not, you will be good for nothing but hard labour in the mines or the fields. For the pittance you'll earn me it's hardly worth the cost of feeding and transporting you. Now, for the love of Tanit,* tell me your name.'

What was he now? Lucius wondered. Not human or animal. Why was he even alive? To be a slave? Surely not. He'd kept himself alive for only one purpose. If he was anything now, he was vengeance. He decided in that instant what to call himself. He would take the name of one of the Furies, the Greek deities of revenge. Through cracked lips, he told Abdosir his new name:

'Alecto.'

* Tanit: the chief goddess of the city of Carthage in North Africa (now part of Tunis in Tunisia).

PART TWO

EXILE

CHAPTER VI

CARTHAGE, NORTH AFRICA
13–14 MARCH AD 82

'Guard position, Alecto!' bellowed Gracchus.

Lucius stood with his feet shoulders' width apart, body turned a shade from full front, knees slightly bent, wooden sword held at waist height. The sun beat down mercilessly on his head as he waited.

'Strike!'

He lunged with his sword straight at the trainer's huge chest.

'Striking air again, Alecto?' sneered Gracchus, who had moved like lightning and now had the tip of his own wooden sword pressed against Lucius's throat. 'Try again... Guard position...

'Strike!'

Lucius struck again, and this time a foot came out of nowhere and sent him sprawling in the dust.

Gracchus looked down at Lucius with his single piercing blue eye. Not for the first time, Lucius found himself wondering what had happened to Gracchus's other eye, now covered with a black patch. Who could possibly have got close enough to this big, fleet-footed veteran to inflict such a wound? Whoever it was deserved a medal.

'Get back on your feet, you tortoise!' barked Gracchus. 'Come on! Look sharp! Guard position...

'Strike!'

As Lucius came swinging, Gracchus darted to one side and sent the flat of his sword slicing towards Lucius's head. Lucius ducked, feeling the sword whistling through his hair. He whirled around, bringing his sword hard into Gracchus's exposed back. The big man stumbled and fell clumsily to his knees. As he was rising, Lucius struck again, this time on his chest, and Gracchus collapsed backwards onto his bottom. Lucius pointed his sword tip at the trainer's chin and began to smile. A second later, his world was violently flipped around, as his legs flew upwards and he crashed cheek-first to the ground. By the time he realised what had happened, he was lying on his back staring down the wrong end of Gracchus's sword.

Frustration, mingled with resentment, made his lips tremble. 'That's not fair,' he complained.

'We call it the Punic* Surprise,' said the trainer. 'It may not be the done thing in Rome, but there's nothing in the rules against tripping up your opponent.' Gracchus put away his sword and gave Lucius a kick in the ribs. 'Get up, boy.'

Lucius clambered to his feet and began to walk away.

'Did I tell you you were dismissed? Get back here!'

Sighing, Lucius returned. His stomach was growling for lunch.

Gracchus leaned in close, so Lucius could smell the goat and onion stew on his breath. 'You've been with us six months now,' said Gracchus, 'and you're not much better than the day you arrived. You've learnt a few moves with the sword, sure. But anyone can do that. That's not what makes a gladiator. I threw my money away on you, boy, that's for sure. I might as well have bet on an oxcart winning at the Carthage Circus.'**

I'm not a fighter, Lucius wanted to say. *I'm not my brother. I wasn't born for this life.* But what was the use? Gracchus was made of stone. The man had no humanity. Lucius was just an investment to him – a failing investment.

---

* *Punic: from Carthage.*

** *There was a big circus (racetrack) in Carthage – only 100 yards (90 metres) shorter than the one in Rome.*

When he had arrived in the city of Carthage six months earlier, after a gruelling, week-long journey by land and sea, Lucius had no idea what fate held in store for him, but he never dreamed he'd end up following in his brother's footsteps and training to be a gladiator. His real fear back then was that he'd be doomed to a life of mindless hard labour, digging and ploughing cornfields under a hot North African sun.

'I can read and write,' Lucius had assured Abdosir, the slave dealer. 'Perhaps you could offer my services as a scribe or a clerk. Surely a cultured city like Carthage has need of such people.' But if anyone was hiring scribes or clerks, they weren't bidding high enough for Abdosir.

'I'll be a teacher's assistant then,' pleaded Lucius. 'Or a physician's apprentice…'

But Abdosir, led as always by his love of money, had ignored Lucius's requests and simply sold him to the highest bidder at the slave auction – and the highest bidder happened to be Gracchus, who was seeking new recruits for his gladiator school.

Gracchus had been kind to Lucius in those early weeks. He made sure he ate and slept well, and gave him as much time as he needed with the medicus* until his ankle was fully healed. It was only later that Lucius understood this to be the kindness a farmer shows towards his pigs before leading them to the slaughterhouse.

* *medicus: doctor.*

Lucius had made rapid progress at first, thanks in part to his experience of watching the gladiators train at the Ludus Romanus* back in Rome. He threw himself into the physical exercises, and as the weeks went by his lean frame began to acquire a thick layer of muscle. Gracchus watched with satisfaction as Lucius attacked the palus** with his sword for hour after hour, cutting, thrusting, stabbing and parrying. He learned the vulnerable points at which to strike, and quickness in recovery from the strike to the guard position. 'You're going to make me a fortune,' Gracchus swore, baring his yellow teeth in an alarming grin.

The lanista decided that Lucius should be a Hoplomachus – a gladiator equipped to resemble a Greek heavy infantryman, or hoplite. That meant he had to wear an all-enclosing bronze helmet; a small round shield; a manica, or metal armguard, on his right arm; leg wrappings and greaves (shin armour). His weapons were a spear and a short sword.

It was when Gracchus started pairing Lucius with other fighters in practice bouts that things started to go wrong. However competent Lucius had become at fighting a wooden post, he was next to useless when confronted by a human opponent. Constantly out-thought, outwitted and out-manoeuvred, he would almost always end up sitting or lying in the dust with a sword at his throat. As Gracchus watched his young

* Ludus Romanus: Roman school (of gladiators).
** palus: a wooden post planted in the ground, used as a target for sword practice.

115

star fail time and again, the kindly twinkle soon faded from his one eye, and his grin contorted into a snarl. He became indignant, as if Lucius had somehow deceived him into thinking he was better than he was.

'I should cut my losses and demote you to Gregarius,' muttered Gracchus as he rose to his feet.

Lucius shuddered. Gregarii were the lowliest type of gladiator – they usually fought in groups and were little more than fodder for wild beast shows or battle re-enactments, unlikely to survive more than a single bout.

The lanista wiped arena dust from his hands. 'Training session's over. Now get out of my sight.'

After a quick wash, Lucius made his way to the dining hall of the ludus. He sat at a table on his own, ignoring the shouts and laughter of the other gladiators as he spooned down his meal of barley gruel, beans and bone ash. He'd not made any friends since coming here, and nor did he wish to. He hated Gracchus, he hated this whole place. As soon as he could, he'd escape from the school, stow himself aboard the next Rome-bound ship and fulfil his life's true mission: to track down and kill the people who had murdered his father and brother.

His desire to break out of the ludus was like an urgent pressure on his heart – and now, with Gracchus's threat to make him a Gregarius still ringing in his ears, it was becoming overwhelming. But with the dormitories locked each night, and guards permanently posted on the gates, it seemed an impossible dream. Yet he knew that if he didn't escape soon, he would die here, and so would his mission of vengeance.

When he returned to the training ground that afternoon, Lucius was in for a shock.

'I'm putting you down for a fight in the spectacle tomorrow,' Gracchus told him. 'Grumio injured himself this morning, so you're going to take his place.'

Lucius's mouth dropped open. 'You actually want me to…?'

The idea of facing a real opponent with real weapons filled him with terror.

'Stop gurning like a fish and get over to the practice arena,' snapped Gracchus. 'Trogus is waiting to fight you. You'd better show some improvement, boy, if you're not going to embarrass us all in the amphitheatre.'

Lucius raced over to the small, oval practice arena. Trogus was already kitted out in the outfit of a Murmillo – similar to a Hoplomachus but with a large rectangular shield and no spear. They would be fighting, as usual, with wooden swords, weighted with iron to make them as heavy as real ones – Gracchus didn't want to risk serious injury to his expensive gladiators in a training bout.

Trogus was a big, heavy fellow – a tiro* like Lucius, but far ahead of him in Gracchus's pecking order, having won most of his training bouts. Several of his friends were sitting on the wooden benches ready to cheer him on. No one was supporting Lucius, of course. He didn't know what the gladiators and staff thought of him – this silent, aloof character who spoke to no one. He couldn't even earn their grudging respect, because he had yet to win a single bout. He was probably something of a joke figure in the ludus – not that he cared much what they thought.

Lucius hated wearing his visored helmet. It restricted his vision and gave him a breathless, panicky feeling of being trapped in a tiny space, making the whole fighting experience even more horrible. Watching through his eye holes, he tried to keep Trogus in sight as they circled each other. Lucius had his spear raised in his right hand, its point directed at Trogus's heart. Remembering his training, he tried to keep his upper body taut and motionless, giving away no hint of his intentions, while at the same time watching his opponent's arms and shoulders for any sign of an impending lunge. It was hard, though, because Trogus kept his sword hidden behind his big shield, so Lucius couldn't see his planned angle of attack.

---

* *tiro: beginner; a gladiator who has never fought in public before.*

Lucius decided his best hope was to go on the offensive. He made a sudden feint, jerking his spear towards Trogus's helmet, but Trogus didn't fall for it – and when Lucius's real attack came, a swift cut from the sword in his left hand, Trogus moved swiftly to parry it with his own. Then Trogus moved in to the attack with a shield charge that struck Lucius on the arm, throwing him off balance. The bigger boy stepped in, stabbing hard at Lucius's side before leaping back. There were cheers from Trogus's friends in the stands. If the weapons had been real, that move would have drawn blood.

Lucius tried to stay calm. He decided, once again, to go on the attack and launched into a flurry of well-rehearsed moves involving spear thrusts and sword strikes. Trogus dealt with the assault easily with a fluid series of blocks, retreats and counter-stabs. During one such move, Trogus let his shield move too far from his body. Spotting an opening, Lucius leaned in and tried to drive his spear down over the shield towards Trogus's chest. As he did so, Trogus smashed the shield into Lucius's face, stepping forward and stabbing at the same time. It had been a trap! Lucius was knocked backwards onto the ground, dazed by the shield bash to his cheek. When he looked up, Trogus had his sword tip pressed to Lucius's gullet. The cheers were half-hearted – Trogus's friends had hoped for a longer, more exciting fight.

'Use the Punic Surprise!' yelled Gracchus, who had

just arrived. But Trogus danced out of the way before Lucius could even think about tripping him up. After removing his helmet, Trogus helped Lucius to his feet. His face showed no sign of exertion.

'Congratulations,' Lucius said weakly.

Trogus didn't reply. Instead, he went straight up to Gracchus: 'I hope you can find me a stronger opponent to practise with before the spectacle tomorrow.'

He probably hadn't meant Lucius to hear this, but the words stabbed at an already raw wound. Lucius knew he was an inept fighter, but he hated hearing it confirmed. What had come so naturally to Quin clearly didn't to him. Yet he had probably trained and exercised harder than any other tiro at the ludus. He was as fit as a horse, with a muscular physique that any young tiro would be proud of – in fact, he barely recognised himself from the scrawny, limping boy who had arrived here six months ago. But there was obviously something missing in him that no amount of exercise could put right. He wished he could work out what that something was – otherwise he was almost certainly going to get killed at the spectacle.

The amphitheatre was packed to capacity, with thirty thousand excited, cheering spectators. The crowd represented almost every stratum of Carthaginian society, from the governor of the province down to the lowliest freedman. But to Lucius, standing at the entry gate waiting to come on, they were all just a single blurred mass of movement and noise. He was standing at one end of the oval arena. The limestone perimeter walls on either side had barred gates set within them from which animals could be introduced. Statues of gods and goddesses looked down from perches atop the wall. The largest of these was a magnificent sculpture of the goddess Juno Caelestis,* patron of the city. At the far end of the oval, some 175 paces away, slaves dressed as underworld gods were carrying the corpse of a defeated gladiator through the Gate of Death.

Save me a place on the ferry across the Styx, my friend, thought Lucius bleakly.

In the centre of the arena, the victorious gladiator stood with his arm raised, holding up his victory palm, acknowledging the cheers of the crowd. Meanwhile, more slaves were busy raking away the bloodied sand and sprinkling fresh white sand in its place.

Any moment now, Lucius would have to go on. The shaft of his spear felt slippery in his hand. He wiped the sweat off onto his loincloth and took a firmer grip. The spear tip gleamed with an evil sharpness, reminding him once again that this fight would be for real. He made a practice jab, then reached with his other hand for his sword, tucked in its leather scabbard. In his mind, he went through the moves. He knew

---

* *Juno Caelestis Heavenly Juno – the Roman name for the Carthaginian goddess Tanit.*

them so well by now, they had become instinctive, like writing his name on a wax tablet.

He pulled the sword a little way out so he could gaze once more at its razor edge – that edge he would shortly try to cut flesh with – and he remembered something his brother had once said: 'The first time you face naked steel in anger is a moment that stays with you for the rest of your life.'

How many times had Quin stood here at the arena entrance, waiting to come on – but Quin had always been blessed with an inner confidence. He believed he could beat anyone – and it was true, he could! He proved it time and again. Even when it seemed as though he'd met his match, he always managed to find something extra. Where did it come from, that supreme confidence? Was he touched by the gods? Lucius closed his eyes and silently mouthed an entreaty to his brother's shade. *Give me some of your strength, brother, so that I may survive this day, and live to avenge you.*

At last the victorious gladiator departed, giving a nod to Lucius as he passed him at the gate. An attendant touched Lucius's arm. 'It's time,' he said, handing him his helmet. Lucius felt a sickening emptiness, as if a dark chasm had opened up beneath his feet. For the first time he noticed his opponent, standing to his right. He was a Thraex or Thracian, a traditional opponent of the Hoplomachus. Lucius had faced many of them in practice bouts, and had lost each and every time. This one was facing front, ignoring Lucius.

Armed with a foot-long, curved dagger, the Thraex was protected by a small, rectangular shield, padded arm and thigh guards, and greaves. He had a bandage around his chest, presumably from an injury sustained in a previous bout. His head was obscured by a visored, wide-brimmed helmet decorated by a griffin, the symbol (as Lucius couldn't help recalling) of impending doom. The Thraex was not big – in fact he was smaller than Lucius – but he looked agile and confident as he rolled his shoulders and stretched his leg muscles.

Lucius tried to swallow, and discovered that his throat was completely dry. With shaking hands, he put on his helmet, closing down the outside world to nothing but the view through two small eye holes. His breath came in loud, thudding gasps inside the bronze bowl of his helmet as he and his opponent stepped out onto the arena. They made their way slowly towards the governor's box, and Lucius hardly felt the scorching sun on his bare shoulders. The burning tightness in his stomach was far, far worse.

An official formally presented the gladiators to the governor, who was also the giver of the games. Lucius barely listened, his attention drawn instead by a charcoal-filled brazier where an arena slave had heated the tip of an iron rod to a bright orange glow, ready to force reluctant gladiators to fight each other.

No escape! I will have to fight!

A cheer went up from a section of the crowd at the mention of his opponent's name: Tycho. The crowd was informed that Tycho was a veteran with three victories behind him.

Dazed by this, Lucius wondered what Gracchus was thinking of, pairing him with someone so experienced. Did he want him killed?

Then the truth dawned: yes, that was exactly what Gracchus wanted. He was cutting his losses – he'd decided Lucius wasn't even worth demoting to Gregarius. Death was the quickest and cleanest solution to the problem of his failed investment. No more having to feed, clothe and shelter him. And at least this way he'd be paid by the organisers of the games: even the lowliest gladiator, killed at the most minor spectacle, had to be paid for.

When the name of Alecto was called, the cheering was much more muted, even though he was the 'local boy'. There were some murmurs of surprise – and a few gasps of excitement – when the crowd learned that a tiro was being paired against a veteran. Although gladiator fans appreciated fights between well-matched opponents, sometimes they also enjoyed a bit of mindless slaughter, which was what this match appeared to promise. Lucius sensed that the feverish betting taking place in the stands above him was not about who would win, but how long the fight would last.

He raised his arm to salute the governor, and noticed with surprise that his hand was no longer shaking. For some reason, he was feeling less nervous. No one expected him to survive more than five minutes – well, maybe he could do a little better than that. After all, he had nothing to lose. If his life was now measurable in minutes, then Gracchus was no longer important, and nor was anything else. All that mattered was what lay right in front him, here in this little oval of sand. And the power to decide his fate was now in his own hands. 'It's like nothing on earth,' Quin once said to him, describing these moments in the arena. 'You feel the power of emperors and the freedom of birds, and it's all yours, simply by surrendering to the moment.'

The summa rudis, or chief referee, called for the fight to begin. Lucius began to circle Tycho, trying to assess the nature of the young man he faced. But Tycho advanced on him with unexpected swiftness, seemingly determined to end the fight before it had even properly started. For a second, Lucius panicked as sharpened steel threatened to slice him in two. Then the training kicked in: he took a step backwards and raised his sword to block. The edge of Tycho's curved sword hammered down on his gladius with the loud ring of a blacksmith's workshop, startling Lucius, who was used to the hollow thwock of wood on wood. He felt his legs buckle under the force, but he recovered quickly and tried to counter with a spear strike beneath Tycho's shield. His opponent swayed with the flexibility of a snake, avoiding the spear, while slicing his sword downwards towards Lucius's thigh. Lucius quickly spun out of harm's way.

After this aggressive opening, Tycho seemed content to stand off for a bit, and they circled each other at a distance of about six paces. Too late, Lucius realised Tycho's trick – he was turning him in order to get the sun in his eyes. Half-blinded by the glare, Lucius sensed a blur of movement in front of him. He rushed forward to meet his opponent's charge, bringing up his shield and jabbing wildly with his spear. He connected with nothing, but felt a sharp slash across his ribs. There was hardly any pain, and he was shocked to feel the warm trickle of blood on his skin.

'Habet!' cried the spectators. 'He's taken one!'

Lucius didn't look at the wound, not daring to let Tycho out of his sight even for a second – but he could tell it was minor. He'd been lucky this time. His instinctive counterattack had left him badly exposed. He could so easily have been killed.

On the positive side, he was still here – probably confounding a few spectators' predictions. The longer he stayed in this fight, the better, he reckoned, were his chances. Tycho was agile, but quite small. Lucius had a longer reach, and maybe he could use that to his advantage. His mistake just now had been to get in too close – he had to try and keep his distance while attacking.

Lucius advanced cautiously, trying to distract Tycho with some impressive swinging of his sword while waiting for an opening to use his spear. The sun flashed dramatically on the steel as it sliced through the air. He remembered Gracchus's words: *Keep your elbows bent, and close to your body. Extend your sword, not your arms.* When he was within a couple of paces of Tycho, he began his attacks – cutting, stabbing and slicing. From this range, his opponent could block and parry, but his counterstrikes could not hope to find their target. As this was going on, Lucius was constantly looking for an opportunity for his spear, but Tycho, all too aware of this lurking danger, kept his shield raised across his unarmoured torso.

Lucius attacked with energy and vigour, pleased that all his exercising had paid off in terms of stamina – he wasn't tired, just hot and sweaty. For the first time in the fight, he felt a measure of control. The crowd had become muted – this wasn't going as expected. There were even some throaty cheers from the few who enjoyed the sight of an unknown tiro doing well.

But then, in the middle of one of his smoothly executed manoeuvres, his opponent made a sudden, unexpected sidestep, and Lucius lost his balance. As he slipped, he felt a sharp blow that struck his right arm. If it hadn't been for his manica, it would have taken the limb clean off. Instead, it just knocked him off his feet. As he tumbled into the dust, he realised that the feeling of control had been an illusion – the Thraex had been playing him along.

These were always the most dangerous moments in any fight. Lucius went into a desperate roll before Tycho could leap on top of him and pin him to the ground. When he regained his feet, he had a moment of dizziness. He couldn't see Tycho anywhere! He whirled this way and that, cursing his helmet for its restricted view. The statue of Juno Caelestis swung into view. Her eyes seemed to flash a warning of an impending attack. Whether he was inspired by the goddess or his own instinct, his next action saved his life. He swung his sword in a wide arc behind him. It struck Tycho's shield just as the Thraex was launching a killing blow to Lucius's back.

Tycho was knocked aside, but swiftly resumed his attack with a devastating strike to Lucius's helmet. Lucius staggered about, ears ringing, but was given no time to recover, for he was immediately subjected to a sustained sequence of rapid assaults from all directions. Tycho became a whirling demon, a blur of murderous violence. Like the many-headed hydra, that deadly serpent of Greek legend, he seemed to attack from different places at once. Lucius was frantically blocking with his shield while simultaneously parrying with his spear. He ducked and swerved and flinched and stumbled while all the time being driven back and back. This was the end, surely! Deafened by his own frenzied breathing, dazzled by the pain of the unending, wrist-breaking blows from his opponent's sword, he just wanted it to be over. His spear finally snapped under yet another skull-bound strike, and a heartbeat later his back collided heavily with the perimeter wall, knocking all the breath out of him.

He slid to the ground in a daze, and felt the point of Tycho's Thracian sword digging into his chest.

Lucius tried to catch his breath. His head hurt. His wrist hurt. Everything hurt! He could feel blood flowing from his side and also from his leg – he must have picked up another wound without even realising it. From somewhere above came a faint cry: 'Punic Surprise!' This was greeted with laughter – obviously it was a well-known local trick. Tycho was standing over Lucius, astride his ankles. Lucius might have been able to summon the strength to trip him – turn the tables on the Thraex, who was obviously not from around here – but he couldn't bring himself to attempt it. Even with his life now hanging by a thread, he just couldn't do something so deceitful. Instead, he raised the index finger of his left hand, calling on the summa rudis to stop the fight. The crowd immediately erupted into cries of 'Iugula! Iugula!' ('Kill! Kill!') and 'Mitte!' ('Let him go!'). From inside the echo chamber of Lucius's helmet, the voices favouring death seemed much louder.

They don't even know me, these people, he reflected miserably, *yet they want me dead.* He'd heard Gracchus speak scathingly of the Carthaginian fight fans – 'bloodthirsty savages' was his term for them them, and he added that this was no more than could be expected of a people who used to sacrifice children to their gods. Luckily, the decision did not rest with them. Lucius tilted his gaze towards the governor's box. The governor had risen to his feet, but had yet to make any signal. He was a tall man, a native of Rome from his complexion – thoughtful-looking, with creases of anxiety or weariness in his face. He didn't seem comfortable in the role he'd been assigned. In some ways, he reminded Lucius of his father. Lucius prayed that the governor might share his father's distaste for meaningless slaughter.

He could still feel the tip of Tycho's long, curved blade pressed painfully against his chest. If he tilted his neck upwards, he could see its deadly gleam against the blue sky. In the next few seconds, six inches of that metal might go ploughing through his ribcage to pierce his heart. These might be the final sights and sounds of his life. He wished he could kiss his father's ring, but he hadn't been allowed to wear it for the fight.

The cries of the crowd grew louder and more restive. They were becoming impatient for a decision. Finally, the governor held up his hand, but Lucius couldn't see it properly for the tears that starred his vision. The groans of the crowd gave him a clue. He blinked, and saw that the governor's thumb was covered – the sign for mercy.

He couldn't move. He heard his breathing taking on a steadier rhythm, felt his muscles start to relax, but he still couldn't believe he'd actually been spared. The crowd didn't seem able to believe it, either. Angry shouts and hisses ricocheted around the amphitheatre. The governor looked pale and shaky as he retook his seat, as if already beginning to regret his decision.

The pressure of the sword tip was lifted from Lucius's chest. He felt a hand grasp his own and help him to his feet. It was Tycho. He gave Lucius a friendly pat on the shoulder.

I'm still alive, Lucius told himself, disbelievingly. And his next thought was: *Now I must get out of here. The gods have spared me for a reason. Somehow, I have to escape!*

In the seats reserved for members of the local ludus, Lucius spotted Gracchus. The lanista looked as annoyed as most of the rest of the crowd that his young tiro had been spared – this scenario had clearly not been part of his calculations.

An attendant handed Tycho his palm of victory, which he raised aloft in triumph. The crowd had, by now, regained its celebratory mood and loudly cheered the Thraex. Tycho began to remove his helmet, and Lucius was happy to be able to do the same.

Wiping the sweat from his brow, he turned and looked with curiosity at his former adversary, now revealed… and that was when he got the shock of his life.

To everyone in the crowd, the Thraex had the appearance of a young man. Only Lucius knew she was, in fact, a girl. Her dark hair was cropped short, and her complexion was darker than he remembered, but there was no mistaking those familiar features.

'Isidora!' he couldn't help shouting.

Isi turned, and her velvety brown eyes seemed to grow impossibly wide.

'Lucius!'

CHAPTER VII

14–15 MARCH

Lucius was in a state of shock. From Isi's expression, it seemed that she was, too. A thousand questions burned in his brain. How could his old friend – whom he had seen off nearly two years ago as she boarded a ship bound for her homeland of Egypt – have ended up fighting in an arena in Carthage? What had happened to her dream of leading a life of freedom and tranquillity on the banks of the Nile? And how could she – *she!* – possibly have got away with posing as a male gladiator?

Before he got the chance to ask her any of these things, Isi was ushered forward to the governor's box to receive his congratulations, while Lucius was gently but firmly steered towards the arena exit. As he was being led away, he turned back, desperate to catch her eye. Isi was also looking back towards him. She mouthed something that he couldn't understand. Straight after that he was led through the exit and she was lost from sight.

Back at the ludus, Lucius asked the medicus treating his wounds if he knew anything about the mysterious Thraex he had faced today. The medicus didn't, but he suggested Lucius try speaking to Zeno, one of the school's coaches, whose job was to assess the opposition for the lanista. As soon as his sword cuts had been dressed, Lucius went straight to Zeno's tiny office on the upper floor, next door to Gracchus's much larger one. Lucius hoped Gracchus wasn't about – the lanista hated seeing gladiators in the administrative section of the ludus. He knocked quietly on Zeno's door, and was immediately invited in.

Zeno was a small man with a bony face surrounded by thick, dark curls. His mouth expanded into a wide grin when he saw the bandaged Lucius enter. 'I wasn't expecting to see you walk off that arena in one piece, young man,' he chuckled. 'Your fate looked sealed once the crowd started calling for death. You have to thank the governor, although I'm not sure even he knows why he decided to make himself so unpopular by granting you life. I told Gracchus from the start that it was a ludicrous pairing, but he wouldn't listen to me. I suspect he wanted to see you dead just so he could collect the compensation money.' Zeno slid his eyes towards the wall that divided his office from Gracchus's and put a finger to his smirking lips. 'Don't tell him I said that, will you?'

'Of course I won't,' said Lucius. 'Um, Zeno, I'm interested in my opponent today. Can you tell me anything about her, I mean him – like which school he's with?'

Zeno twinkled mischievously. 'Why do you want to know, Alecto? Thinking of inflicting a little private revenge for the beating you got today?'

Lucius didn't know Zeno well, but what he did know made him distrust the man. He was a gossip by nature, and he encouraged those around him to be just as indiscreet. No doubt it helped him in his job – seeking out juicy tidbits about the gladiators in other ludi – but it also meant that whatever Lucius said to him now was bound to get back to Gracchus, and he didn't want the lanista, or anyone else, to know that he knew Isidora. It could lead to awkward questions about his past, and someone might end up guessing his real identity. As far as the authorities were aware, Lucius had died in the Pontine Marshes, and he very much wanted to keep things that way. After all, being officially dead could prove a vital advantage if he ever managed to get back to Rome to carry out his mission of revenge.

'I–I'm just curious,' he said.

Zeno arched his eyebrows and nodded slowly in a manner that suggested he didn't believe Lucius. He consulted a scroll on his desk, running his finger down a list of names. 'You know of course that contact with gladiators outside this school is strictly prohibited?'

'Yes, of course.'

'Ah, here,' said Zeno, his eye picking out the name on the list. 'Tycho isn't attached to a ludus. He's a member of a troupe of travelling fighters known as the Swords of Isis. I had a chat with their lanista at the Cena Libera* last night, a very nice chap by the name of Hierax. They're due to ship out to Corinth tomorrow on the morning tide. So if you are planning to sneak out of here and cut the boy's throat, you'd better do so tonight!'

That evening, Lucius dined alone as usual. He wouldn't have been able to speak to anyone anyway in his current miserable state. It wrenched at his heart that Isidora would be leaving the city tomorrow. What terrible luck to have caught a glimpse of his friend, only for her to slip away again. And to Corinth, in Greece! – half a world away. Had fate really brought them together, only to tear them apart again so quickly? He

---

* Cena Libera: free feast – a banquet given for the gladiators the night before their performance.

had to break out of here tonight and try to find her. Zeno had refused to say where her troupe was staying, but if it was their last night here, he was bound to find some of these 'Swords of Isis' fellows drinking in one of the city's taverns or gaming houses. He could then follow them back to their camp. That was the easy part. The hard part was getting out of the ludus.

He heard laughter from another table, and looked up to see Gracchus with his arm around Trogus, the Murmillo, who had won impressively today. Gracchus hadn't said a word to Lucius since the fight, and he wondered what the lanista had in mind for him. Did he plan to send him out against another stronger opponent tomorrow in the hope that this time Lucius might do the decent thing and get himself killed? Or perhaps he intended to sell him at auction – a common fate for defeated gladiators. Lucius didn't intend to stay and find out.

But how could he get out of here? The Auctorati – the volunteer gladiators – were allowed out on a regular basis, but slave-gladiators like him were permanently confined to barracks. He'd heard that the guards were susceptible to bribes, and some of the more successful veteran slave-gladiators would often pay the guards to go temporarily blind and deaf, so they could get out of the ludus and celebrate their latest victory with a night on the town. But Lucius had no money for bribes, and no influential friends to help him.

All he could hope for was a little compassion...

'Melus,' Lucius said to the burly old guard standing outside the door of his cell – he was pleased that he remembered the man's name. 'I haven't been out of this place in six long months. I fought my first fight today – and very nearly died. I'd really like to go out tonight and see the city. Do you think that might be possible? I know you've arranged it for some of the other lads in here.'

Melus frowned at him, then glanced discreetly in both directions to see if anyone was coming down the corridor. When he was satisfied that no one was about, he said in a low voice: 'The price is 40 sestertii. That includes payment for the guards at the gate.'

'I don't have any money,' confessed Lucius helplessly.

'D'you have anything of value?' asked Melus, eyeing the chalcedony ring on his finger.

'No,' said Lucius, covering the ring protectively with his hand. 'Nothing I can offer you. I was hoping you might do this for me as an act of charity. I'll owe you a big favour for this.'

He searched for signs of compassion in the man's unshaven face, but Melus only grinned, revealing a set of mostly rotten or missing teeth. 'Favours from gladiators ain't a currency I recognise, young man,' he said. 'They only last as long as the gladiators who owe them, and gladiators don't tend to last long, if you take my meaning…'

With that, Melus clanged the cell door shut. Lucius threw himself onto his straw mattress, his mind as dark and dismal as his surroundings. He closed his eyes until he felt the beginnings of a pain-numbing drowsiness steal over him – but he knew he couldn't fall asleep without first performing his nightly ritual.

Near his bed, in the glow of the room's single oil lamp, was a small shrine he had made to his father's shade. He raised himself up from his mattress and kneeled before it. The shrine consisted of a shallow wooden crate, once used for transporting fruit, which he'd found on a rubbish heap in the yard behind the kitchen. He had placed this on its side and set within it a wax-tablet portrait of his father's likeness – the best he could render from memory. Alongside the tablet, he placed the statue of the little wooden dog – his father's favourite of their household deities – which had somehow survived Lucius's fall into the marshes, and everything that had happened since. Next to the dog were some sticks of incense – the gift of a departing gladiator, who had bought himself free not long after Lucius's arrival. He had given incense to every gladiator at the ludus, intending it to be used in the worship of Fortuna, his favourite goddess. Next to the sticks Lucius had placed a small jug of olive oil and a bowl, which Lucius had taken from a table in the dining hall.

Lucius took off his ring and kissed it before placing it next to the dog statuette. He lit the incense, breathing in its scent while focusing on the wax image of Aquila. He poured a little of the oil into the bowl as an offering, then clasped his hands. 'Father,' he murmured, 'grant me the strength to survive these days, and the wisdom to make the right choices. Please watch over Valeria, and see that she is safe. I pray that she is with Mother and that they are both in good health. I pray also that Quintus has found his way safely across the Styx, and is with you... Father, I have asked for your advice many times, I know, and I know you cannot give it to me in words. But perhaps you could give me a sign to prove that you are here still and that I am not entirely alone and abandoned... May the gods bless your spirit and keep you safe.'

Lucius bowed his head and prayed silently for a moment, mouthing words of thanks to the gods – particularly Juno Caelestis, who had saved his life today, but also Cybele, for disguising him during the escape from the Praetorians, and Antheia, for protecting him in the marshes. Then he blew out the lamp, crept back to bed and curled up tight, waiting for sleep to carry him away, at least temporarily, from his sorrows.

'Alecto!' The harsh whisper echoed in the darkness. 'Wake up, young man!'

Lucius stirred. He blinked and sat up. 'What is it?' he called.

His cell door stood open and a dim light filled the room. Melus stood there, his bulky, stooping figure filling the doorway. 'You have a visitor,' he grinned. 'A young man who understands better than yourself the lubricating effects of money. It oils the wheels, my friend.'

Lucius started breathing very fast. He staggered to his feet as Melus stood aside and Isi came into the room. A warm shiver of joy ran through Lucius when he saw her. Without saying a word, they hugged each other.

'Isi,' he whispered.

'Shhh,' she said in a voice that was lower than he remembered, 'I'm Tycho.' Then, with a suppressed giggle, she added: 'And you're, er, Alecto.'

Isi took his hand and tugged him towards the door. 'Let's go.'

'Go?' Lucius couldn't believe his ears. He glanced at Melus, but the guard didn't seem concerned.

'Remember,' Melus said to Isi in the same friendly tone: 'bring him back before sunrise, or I'll hunt you both down and feed you to the lions in the amphitheatre.'

'Of course!' vowed Isi.

Lucius's heart was beating so loudly, he was

surprised the others couldn't hear it. Was he really getting out of here – with Isi?

He began to reach for his sack of meagre possessions, but stopped when he realised that taking it would look suspicious. Instead – as casually as he could – he slid the ring onto his finger and stuffed the dog statuette into his belt-pouch. Everything else was replaceable.

'Go quickly,' said Melus. 'The porter has had to pay a visit to the latrine, but he will be back shortly.'

As Lucius followed Isi down the corridor on legs shaking with excitement, she whispered to him: 'These guards were very expensive. I had to give them all my winnings from today's fight to spring you out of here.' She stopped and grabbed his arm suddenly, pulling him round to face her. He saw the glint of a tear in her eye. 'I'm glad that money's gone,' she said, her voice shaking. 'I feel sick that I nearly killed you today. If I'd known it was you, I'd have…'

Lucius shook his head. 'Don't think about it,' he said. 'How could you possibly have known?'

The exterior door of the ludus was, as Melus predicted, unguarded when they reached it. They slipped out into the street, and Lucius couldn't help laughing as he breathed the warm night air.

'Run!' shouted Isi.

They ran, even though they didn't need to, and for Lucius it was a glorious release of pent-up tension. He felt his blood pounding in his ears and his limbs pumping away beneath him as they sprinted across a cobbled concourse, past the ludus and the huge curving grey wall of the amphitheatre.

They ran east through narrow streets towards the city centre, until they reached a small square. Here, panting for breath, they stopped and washed their faces in a fountain. The place was lively, even at this late hour. Taverns threw out their light and laughter onto the street, goods wagons squeaked along the pebbled streets, dogs barked, young couples walked along arm in arm, signwriters called to each other as they painted their slogans on the walls, and stern-faced legionaries tramped the streets on the lookout for trouble.

Lucius had seen very little of Carthage before tonight, and now, clothed in moonlight, it looked exotic – familiar, yet strange. The legionaries on patrol were a reminder of home, as were the white marble temples and basilicas visible high above them on Byrsa Hill. But the faces carved on the statues, the dark complexions of the people, the whole hot, humid, perfume-scented night – it was all so foreign and exciting to his senses.

'What now?' asked Lucius, once he'd got his breath back.

'Our ship is leaving at dawn, which is in just a few hours,' said Isi. 'You can be on it... if you want.' She looked at him shyly, her face gleaming with perspiration. He couldn't believe that this nervous-looking girl was the same demonic Tycho who had come within an inch of killing him in the arena that afternoon. He also couldn't believe she was offering him a chance to escape forever from Gracchus and the ludus.

'By all the gods, Isi, do you mean it?' he cried, seizing her hand.

Her face broke into a smile of relief. 'Of course I do. Our lanista, Hierax, is as lovely a boss as you could ever wish for, and I just know he'll welcome a talented fighter like yourself into our ranks. I can't wait to introduce you to him!'

Lucius looked down when she said this, his cheeks burning. 'Don't mock me, Isi. After all we've been through together, I'd expect some honesty from you. You know I'm useless.'

Isi stared at him as if he was mad. 'Are you serious?' she said. 'Don't you know how good you are?' She looked into his eyes and must have glimpsed all the self-doubt he carried within him, because she shook her head sadly. 'You don't, do you? Well, let me tell you something, Lucius, and this is the truth: technically, you're one of the most gifted gladiators I've ever seen – and that includes your brother. The only thing you're lacking – and I admit this is a big, big thing – is fire.'

'What do you mean?'

Isi stared at him with an intensity that he found uncomfortable. It reminded him of their very first meeting, back at the Ludus Romanus. Even then she'd been unbelievably direct. 'I want to know what you are,' she'd demanded of him that day. She was a slave girl then, but she'd spoken to him as an equal. Isi gazed at him now with the same fierce light in her eyes. 'When you were fighting me today,' she said, 'you did everything right. You didn't put a foot wrong, technically. But you had no fire. You didn't want to kill me... If you're going to succeed as a gladiator, you have to hate your opponent – you have to want to kill him.'

'I don't want to hate – or to kill,' muttered Lucius.

Isi sighed, and her gaze fell away. 'Nor do I, but it's a trick I've had to learn.' She lapped the water in the fountain idly with her fingers. In the distance a voice echoed through the streets, calling the fourth watch of the night.

'Actually, if you want the truth,' said Isi with a sad chuckle, 'I always think of your uncle Ravilla and how he killed my parents. I'm afraid I was imagining you as Ravilla today.'

Lucius shook his head in wonder at the change in his friend. He would never have imagined her taking this path. 'Isi, you have to tell me your story – I mean how you came to be a gladiator. I got the shock of my life when I saw you today.'

'Me, too,' she smiled. Then she stood up. 'Of course I'll tell you everything, but first I want you to come with me.'

'Where to?'

'We've got a couple of hours until our ship sails. Before we leave, I want to show you something – something you'll never forget.'

CHAPTER VIII

15 MARCH

Isi pulled Lucius to his feet and led him out of the square and up a steep road. 'This is Byrsa Hill,' she explained, 'the ancient citadel of Carthage.'

They reached the top of the hill and entered the Forum. The great square was dominated by a huge statue of the goddess Juno Caelestis, enthroned on a lion. Isi glanced behind her to be sure they weren't being watched, then levered herself up onto the statue's pedestal.

'Come on!' she called to Lucius as she began scrambling up the lion's gigantic mane. Lucius was startled by her sacrilegious behaviour – if caught, they could be in serious trouble. Also, hadn't this goddess saved his life earlier today? Isi perched herself on the lion's shoulder. Her face glowed like marble in the moonlight, and the night breeze swelled her cloak. To Lucius, she appeared every bit as iconic as the goddess looming above her. She peered through the sculpted tufts of mane at something Lucius couldn't see but which filled her eyes with tears. His anxiety was quickly overwhelmed by curiosity, and he clambered up the statue to join her.

Seated beside Isi, Lucius immediately saw what had moved her. The view from up here on the lion's head took his breath away. The whole of Carthage lay spread before them: thousands of rooftops softly gleaming in the moonlight in a gently curving grid that stretched as far as the eye could see, like the tiers of an enormous amphitheatre, gradually descending towards the coast. Beyond lay the sea, the Mare Nostrum,* its calm surface like beaten silver beneath the full moon. The same celestial light twinkled on the waters of the great circular harbour, where hundreds of merchant ships lay moored, and it shone on the marble roofs of the temples. A smell of salt was carried on the breeze, mingled with the heavy, sweet scent of jasmine.

'Just think,' said Isi, 'this city was a great power when Rome was just a hilltop village.'

Lucius had read histories of the Punic Wars, when Rome had battled the Carthaginians for supremacy over a period of more than a hundred years. From

---

* *Mare Nostrum: 'our sea' – a Roman name for the Mediterranean.*

this vantage, with views of the great defensive wall on the landward side and the secure harbour for its fleet, it was easy to imagine how formidable the city must have been.

'It was a quirk of fate that Rome beat Carthage,' said Isi. 'If things had gone a little differently, we'd all be speaking Phoenician.'*

Lucius couldn't let this one go. 'And I'm sure you'd have been a lot happier as a slave of the Carthaginians,' he smirked.

Isi shot him a look. This had always been a point of tension between them: his loyalty to Rome, and her hostility to it. But he could see from the upturned edges of her lips that she wasn't seriously insulted by his comment.

'Fate works in mysterious ways, doesn't it, Lucius?' she said. 'I've thought about you a lot since leaving Rome, and often dreamed of meeting you again, but never imagined it would be as gladiators in the arena!'

His heart skipped a little when she said this. A flush rose in his cheeks and he was pleased the darkness hid this from her view. 'I often thought of you, too,' he murmured.

'My dreams of a happy life in Alexandria didn't work out,' said Isi. 'Ordinary Egyptians saw me as Roman and hated me for it, while the Roman elite treated me like a slave, even though I'm a freedwoman.

---

* *Phoenician: the language of Carthage and its empire. It was a Semitic language, related to Hebrew and Arabic.*

I felt like an outcast, rejected by everyone. My only remaining family was an aunt – my mother's sister. But she was a difficult person to live with, and I grew restless. In the end, I decided to join a touring gladiator troupe, the Swords of Isis.'

'I never pictured you as a gladiator,' said Lucius.

'I know – it's strange,' she sighed. 'But I think Hierax had a lot to do with it. He was the first person I met in Egypt who didn't treat me like a complete outsider or a person of no status. I suppose it's because the Swords are outsiders themselves. Although Hierax is originally from Egypt, the others are just people he's picked up on his travels. Like me, they're all former slaves. In the Swords, everyone's equal. And it's not like being stuck in a ludus – we're free to come and go as we please. We each put a percentage of our winnings into a group fund to pay for travel, accommodation, weapons, all that, and the rest we keep for ourselves. Since joining the Swords, I actually feel in control of my life, and that's quite a new feeling for me!'

'Isi,' said Lucius, wondering how best to phrase his next question. 'Um, there's one thing you haven't quite explained.'

'What's that?'

'Well, I mean… you're a girl, and…'

'You've noticed, then?' she laughed, and slapped him playfully on the leg. 'I know what you mean – but girls can be gladiators as well. Admittedly, we're usually used as novelty acts, before the main event

– paired against each other, or against dwarfs. We're rarely taken seriously as fighters. And that's how I started. But Hierax quickly realised I had talent – he saw I could defeat men. So he took me aside one day and gave me the armour and weapons of a Thraex. He said that from now on my name would be Tycho, and I would fight as a man. That's the other advantage of being part of a touring troupe – when you arrive in a new city, no one knows who you are, so it's easy to keep things secret, even your gender. I had to deepen my voice when speaking to people outside the troupe, and pretend I had a wound on my chest – and cut my hair, of course…' She ran her fingers through her cropped locks.

'You look very nice like that,' said Lucius, his voice tight. He couldn't help noticing that Isi had changed physically since they'd last met – and not just the short hair. She'd developed breasts, which was the reason for the bandage she'd worn in the amphitheatre today.

'Anyway,' she continued, 'it's a great feeling being able to fight at the highest level and earn the respect of the crowd rather than their laughter and mockery. I have a lot to thank Hierax for.'

On the horizon, the undersides of the long purple clouds were now lit by a deep ruby glow.

'It will be dawn soon,' said Isi. 'We should get going.'

They walked down the wide, straight thoroughfare that linked Byrsa Hill to the sea. As they approached the harbour, Lucius could hear the creaking of ropes, the cry of gulls and the songs of dock workers loading up crates of produce. The smell of the sea was sharp in his nostrils, and whetted his appetite for the voyage ahead. They passed through a gate and entered the vast quayside that surrounded the circular harbour. Ionic columns separated each of the ships' berths – at least two hundred of them by Lucius's estimate – giving the appearance of a continuous ring-shaped colonnade. There were ships everywhere: fishing vessels, trading ships, light Liburnians* and heavy warships with huge curving prows and up to three banks of oars. In the middle of the harbour was a circular building that seemed to float on the water. The prows of yet more ships could be seen jutting from earthen slipways all around the base of this artificial island.

Isi led Lucius along the busy quayside, thronged with sailors, merchants, fishermen and dockworkers.

'Ah, there you are, my girl!' called a brawny middle-aged man, standing by the gangplank of a merchant ship. 'I was starting to get worried.' He had a scarred, weatherbeaten face and kind eyes that crinkled when he saw her. The sun, rising over the harbour wall, shone in his long silver hair, tied at the back in a ponytail.

---

* *Liburnians: ships from Liburnia, in present-day Croatia. The Romans regarded the Liburnian sailors as pirates.*

Isi ran over to him and kissed him on the cheek. 'Hierax, I want you to meet my friend and our latest recruit, Lucius.'

Hierax beamed at Lucius. 'Aha! The young Hoplomachus is here! Isi was determined to steal you away from your ludus, and there was nothing I could say to dissuade her. Welcome, friend!' Hierax clasped his arm, making Lucius wince – the man had a mighty grip. Though not tall, his arms and legs bulged with muscle. 'I confess I'm confused about your name,' continued Hierax. 'At the amphitheatre, you were introduced to the crowd as Alecto…'

'Yes, that's my name,' said Lucius, shooting Isi a warning look.

Hierax chuckled knowingly. 'Most of us here are running away from one thing or other. It's a rare gladiator who fights under his birth name. What you call yourself is your business; I'm interested in you as a fighter, and from what I saw yesterday, I think you'll make a useful addition to our troupe. We lack a Hoplomachus, and I was impressed with your style. If you have a shortcoming, it lies in your commitment to the fight and your tactical awareness – but these are things that are easily put right.'

Lucius glowed at the praise, especially when spoken by a man whose wisdom and experience were so evident in his face.

'All aboard!' called a sailor.

Hierax hustled them both up the gangplank, and

Lucius just had time to read the name painted in faded lettering across the ship's stern: *Concordia*.

He was surprised to discover there were only three other gladiators in the troupe: a select bunch indeed! Hierax introduced him to them. Hilarus was a heavily built Secutor with ginger hair and a surly disposition; Felix was a wiry and cheerful young Retiarius of African origin; and Florus was a tall, dark-eyed Provocator with a profile and cheekbones that wouldn't have looked out of place on a statue of Adonis.* Lucius watched as Felix and Isi engaged in friendly banter, and he felt a pang of jealousy. In the old days, back at the Ludus Romanus and the vivarium, it had been just him and Isi against the world. Now she had a familia,** and he'd never seen her so happy. He was glad for her, but also sad that he now had to share her friendship with others.

Mooring ropes were untied and the ship was cast off. Isi, perhaps sensing Lucius's jealousy, led him away from the others and stood with him near the prow. She took his hand as the *Concordia* made its way out of the harbour. Lucius was comforted by the gesture – it almost felt like old times.

---

* Secutor: 'chaser' – a gladiator who wears an enclosed helmet and uses a short sword (gladius); Retiarius: a gladiator who fights with net (rete) and trident; Provocator: 'challenger' – a sword fighter who carries a large shield like an infantry shield; Adonis: in legend, a mortal who was so handsome that Venus, goddess of love, fell in love with him.

** familia: a troupe, or family, of gladiators.

Suddenly remembering Melus, he scanned the quayside for signs of the guard. 'Melus will be going spare by now,' he said.

Isi giggled. 'He'll lose his job, for sure. But the money I paid him should keep him going for a while.'

Lucius couldn't help smiling as he pictured the surprise awaiting Gracchus – he was pleased that the lanista had never made any money out of him. As they left the harbour and entered the open sea, he took in the vista of endless foam-flecked waves and licked at the salty spray that spattered his face – it was the taste of freedom. Above them, the ship's square sail billowed in the sea wind. Sailors clambered about the rigging with the sure-footedness of monkeys, while down on the deck, Hilarus and Florus gently sparred.

'You haven't told me your story yet,' Isi said to Lucius. 'How exactly did you come to be a gladiator in Carthage – and why are you so keen to be called Alecto?'

As the sun rose into a clear blue sky, Lucius told her his sad tale, starting with Apollonius's prophecy and his father's flight to Titus's villa, and ending with Lucius's sale to Gracchus. Even now, six months on, it was painful to recall all the details.

Isi was shocked to hear of Aquila's death. 'I'm so sorry,' she said, squeezing his hand. 'I only met him briefly, but I could tell your father was a noble and decent man.'

'Thanks,' said Lucius, wiping his eye.

'Do you have any idea who this mysterious person was who killed him?'

'The Praetorian commander who captured us claimed he wasn't one of them. The only clue we have is the tattoo on his chest.'

'Do you think your father was killed to avenge Ravilla – or to silence him from talking about the murder of Titus?'

'I wish I knew.' Lucius had thought about this question so often that his head hurt from it. He wished Isi would drop the subject now, but the mystery had got her intrigued.

'You said there was someone else who witnessed Titus's murder. I wonder if they got to him, too. What did you say his name was?'

'Canio.'

'Would that be Galerius Horatius Canio, by any chance?' said a voice behind them.

Lucius spun around, startled that their conversation had been overheard.

Hierax was standing there, exercising his arm muscles by doing lifts with a heavy-looking barrel.

'Yes, that's him,' replied Lucius – then wished he'd kept quiet.

'Have you heard of him, then?' Isi asked Hierax.

'Oh yes,' grunted the lanista, continuing with his exercises. 'Canio was big news a few months ago, according to my friends in Rome. He was arrested for treason, then managed to escape custody before he could be executed. No one knows where he is now, but I've heard rumours that he's living quietly in the city of Ephesus. Why are you interested in him?'

'We're not,' said Lucius quickly.

Isi tugged him closer to the prow, where the crash of waves was loud enough to mask their voices. She cupped her hand to his ear and said: 'I would trust Hierax with my life. He has no more love for Rome than I do. His only loyalty is to the Swords of Isis – and you're one of us now. You can tell him the truth – he'll never betray you.'

Lucius heard the calm certainty in her voice and was reassured. He turned to Hierax, and said: 'I believe Canio was charged with treason because he's carrying some very dangerous information – he was a witness to the murder of the emperor Titus...'

When he heard this, Hierax dropped the barrel. It fell with a loud crash to the deck and rolled until it hit the base of the mast. 'Murder?' he gasped. 'I thought he died of a fever...' He glanced up towards a sailor busy checking knots in the rigging, then gestured for them to follow him. 'I think you two had better step into my office.'

Hierax's 'office' was a tiny cabin in the bow of the ship, which doubled as his sleeping quarters. The furniture consisted of a simple bed and a large chest. The sounds of the sea were muffled in here, and the only clue that they weren't on land was the soft creak of timbers and the gentle rolling sensation beneath them. Hierax seated himself cross-legged on the bare floorboards, and invited them to join him there, then he listened in closed-eyed silence as Lucius retold his story.

When he had finished, Hierax's grey eyes reopened. 'It seems to me,' he said slowly, 'that Canio may be the only person alive who knows who killed Titus and your father – apart, that is, from the killer himself.'

'How can you be sure they were killed by the same person?' queried Lucius.

Hierax shrugged. 'I'm not necessarily saying that the one who poisoned the emperor's sea-hare also wielded the dagger on your poor father. But it's clear to me that the same mind lay behind both murders.'

'But what about the tattoo?' Isi challenged him. 'Doesn't that point to a different motive for the murder of Aquila?'

Hierax shook his head. 'Supporters of Ravilla hated Titus just as much as they did Aquila, after the emperor brought down their hero. The kestrel tattoo makes me even more convinced that the two murders are connected. The only question that remains is the identity of the murderer, and the one man who can answer that question is Galerius Horatius Canio – who is believed to be hiding out in Ephesus.'

'What exactly are you saying?' asked Isi, her body suddenly taut with excitement. She must have seen something in Hierax's craggy smile that Lucius was at a loss to interpret.

'There's a small gladiatorial festival in Ephesus starting on the Kalends of April,'* replied Hierax. 'I wasn't going to bother with it this year, as the purse is usually quite small – but seeing as we're heading to the Aegean** anyway...'

'Do you mean it?' cried Isi, who had clearly become as gripped by the prospect of solving this mystery as Lucius. 'But what about Corinth?'

'Corinth is no more than five days from Ephesus by sea,' said Hierax. 'We can perform at Ephesus and still make it to Corinth in time for the Isthmian Games, which start on the Ides.*** And that should also give you two enough time to seek out Canio.'

In her elation at this news, Isi hugged Hierax, nearly knocking the lanista onto the floor. Looking back at Lucius, she gasped: 'Didn't I tell you he was a brilliant boss!'

Lucius smiled and clenched his fists in grim delight. At last his mission of vengeance could begin...

---

* *festival . . . April: the Artemision, the annual Ephesian festival to Artemis (the city's patron goddess), took place around the end of March or the beginning of April. Kalends: the first of the month.*

** *Aegean: the part of the Mediterranean Sea that lies between Greece and Turkey.*

*** *the Ides: the 13th.*

CHAPTER IX

31 MARCH

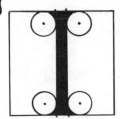 'killed your father!' the man in the helmet growled at Lucius. 'I plunged my dagger deep into his chest and watched as the blood and the life spilled out of him... And I laughed!'

As these words sank in, Lucius turned cold. A roar of anger began inside him that seemed impossible to control. Only his training held him back. He took a firmer grip on his sword, and advanced on his enemy. When he attacked, his body moved with a speed and intensity that only days ago he would have thought impossible. Some part of him remained still and observant in the eye of his own storm, possessed by a cool rage, as his limbs whirled and danced and his blade flickered like a tongue of deadly flame. His blood was up, his skin soaked with sweat, but his heart was cold.

The man in the helmet fought stubbornly, blocking, parrying, always probing for defensive weaknesses; but Lucius was unrelenting, never sacrificing defence for attack, and gradually pushing his opponent backwards.

The man spat more words of hate. 'Your father wept with fear when he saw my dagger. He died like a coward...'

Lucius roared. He attacked with redoubled energy, smashing the man's shield with his own in his determination to get behind it. Finally, the man stumbled. Lucius let out a cheer and went in for the kill. He raised his sword above his head, and... felt a massive blow to his chest.

The air was knocked out of him, and his legs fell away. He looked up from the ship's deck, stunned and blinking as his opponent lifted his sword from Lucius's heart, then removed his helmet and shook out his silver ponytail.

'That was better,' panted Hierax. 'That was much, much better... You nearly had me that time. Just remember... Use the anger, use the hate. But don't be consumed by it.'

'Didn't I tell you you were good?' smiled Isi, helping Lucius to his feet. 'I've not seen anyone put our lanista on the back foot the way you just did.'

Lucius didn't return her smile. He still felt wound

up inside. 'I didn't like the things you said… about my father,' he muttered to Hierax.

The lanista patted him on the back. 'I know, and I'm sorry, son. I won't play that trick again. But I had to do something to put some fire in your belly – just to show you what you're capable of…'

This was their sixteenth day aboard the *Concordia*, and Lucius had spent a good portion of each of those days training with Hierax on the ship's deck. It was only now that he realised how bad a trainer Gracchus had been – bullying and humiliating him rather than teaching Lucius the essential skills, tricks and tactics he needed for man-to-man combat. In just over two weeks, he had learned more about arena fighting than Gracchus had taught him in six months.

'Your opponents won't do for you what I just did,' said Hierax. 'They may shout abuse, but they don't know your history like I do, so what they say won't hurt. But you've got to try and hate them just as much as you hated me just now. You've got to imagine each one of them as your father's killer. If you do that, there won't be a Thraex or Murmillo in the city who'll last five minutes against you.'

'Breakfast!' called the ship's steward.

'Don't tell me,' grumbled Hilarus. 'Salted beef, dried veg and garum sauce, right?'

'How did you guess?' smirked the steward.

They were all thoroughly sick of the food, which was the same each day – but the voyage had been enjoyable in other ways. Lucius need not have feared losing Isi to her new friends – in fact, her friends had simply become his friends as well. They had all welcomed him into the familia – even the gruff Hilarus – and within a few days he'd felt as though he'd known them forever. When not training, they had spent their time competing to see who could kill the most rats – there was an infestation of them in the ship's hold. Hierax had given Lucius a small dagger called a pugio, and he had become adept at throwing it and impaling rats on its blade. In the evenings, Lucius would listen as the others swapped tales of past victories in the arena. He tried not to think too much about Quin and all the tales he might have told, had he been there.

Now, as they sat on deck eating their breakfast, they heard an excited cry from a sailor perched high above them on the spar of the mainsail: 'Ephesus ahead!'

Lucius and Isi dropped their bowls and raced to the front of the ship in time to see the hazy, rocky coastline of Asia Minor* come into view. The watchman above was pointing towards a break in the mountains several miles wide. It was the mouth of an enormous river, lined with sandy beaches and the walls of a harbour. As they drew closer they began to glimpse, beyond the harbour, the whitewashed walls, pillars and red roofs of the Roman city of Ephesus. It lay there, snug and secure between the mountains and the sea – a small patch of home in a vast alien continent.

* *Asia Minor: the Roman name for Anatolia, now part of Turkey.*

The *Concordia* slipped between a pair of ancient watchtowers, leaving behind the foam-capped waves to enter the calmer waters of the harbour. The docks were busy with ships bringing passengers and supplies for the annual festival of Artemision, and they had to wait at anchor for most of the morning until a pilot brought a boat out to guide them in.

After they had docked, Hierax stood with his troupe on the busy quayside and pointed at an impressive pillared edifice standing on a rocky ridge at the foot of a mountain. 'That's the Praetorium, where the governor resides,' he told them. 'Now let your eye run past that to the smaller hill with the two humps – see it?'

Isi nodded. 'It reminds me of one of those Bactrian camels we looked after at the vivarium – remember, Lucius?'

'You may see a few of those beasts on the streets,' said Hierax. 'Traders use them to carry in the spices from the east. Now, in the cleft between the two humps, carved into the hillside, is a huge theatre – you can just see the top of it from here. That's where they hold the gladiator fights.'

'But it's not oval,' observed Felix.

'Well spotted,' said Hierax. 'The Greeks, who built this city, are into arty stuff like drama, and the theatre is really designed for that. If you want the truth, they're a bit snooty about gladiators around here. They think we're a barbaric lot – at least, the city elite do. The ordinary folk of Ephesus love the fights, just as they do everywhere else in the empire. You'll see – the place'll be absolutely packed. But remember, most people speak Greek around here. You won't hear much Latin, so you'll need to get used to the jargon. The games are called *philotimia*, not *munus*. Gladiators are *monomachoi*. If you lose your fight, and the spectators shout *apeluthe*, you're in luck – it means they want to spare you. But if they shout *apokteinon*, it may be the last sound you'll ever hear.'

'Let's hope we're never in that position,' grunted Hilarus.

Lucius drew Hierax to one side. 'How do you suggest we go about finding Canio?' he asked in a low voice.

Hierax scratched a scar on his cheek thoughtfully. 'You should go and see a friend of mine – a fellow by the name of Complexus Ursi, or Ursus for short.* He owns a kapeleion – that's a tavern to you and me – called the Logodrome, close to the agora.** He knows everything that's worth knowing in this city. I usually go to him for the gossip on rival gladiators, but he's full of stories about the Ephesian underworld. If anyone knows where Canio is, it'll be him.'

---

* *Complexus Ursi: bearhug; Ursus: bear.*
** *agora: the Greek word for 'forum' (marketplace).*

'Won't you come with us?' Isi asked.

Hierax shook his head. 'I have to go and see the sponsor of the games and get you lot registered, and also sort out accommodation at the local ludus.' He turned to address the others. 'I'll meet you all at duodecima hora* at the Temple of Artemis, so we can make sacrifice. Ask anyone, they'll tell you where it is. Until then, your time is your own. Show respect to the locals and don't make trouble. And stay clear of the women, Florus! I'll see you all later.'

The lanista strode off, and his troupe were left on their own.

'Anyone speak Greek?' wondered Hilarus.

'I do,' said Isi. 'They speak it a lot in Alexandria.'

'Well, perhaps you can order us all some lunch?' suggested the Secutor, nodding towards a row of fast-food stalls further along the quay.

''Fraid not,' Isi replied with a glance at Lucius. 'Alecto and I have got some important business. Just point at your stomach and show them a coin, Hilly, they'll get the message.'

Felix laughed and guided Hilarus and Florus towards the food stalls. 'Don't worry, Tycho,' he called. 'We'll manage.'

---

* *duodecima hora: the twelfth hour – the last hour of daylight.*

The streets were thronged with excited tourists arriving to celebrate the annual festival of the hunting goddess Artemis, as well as locals seeking to sell them souvenirs. As Isi and Lucius made their way to the city centre, they passed stalls selling figurines of the deity, painted vases, golden hunting bows, stag-shaped cakes of honey and sesame seeds, and models of the famous temple. They had to avoid a herd of goats being led by priests to the temple altar for sacrifice. There was even a miniature theatrical show being performed on a street corner.

At length, they arrived at the Logodrome. It was a shabby, rather ancient establishment that looked as though it had seen better days – or maybe even better centuries. As they entered the dim interior, customers at the small round tables immediately stopped talking and stared at them. There was a smell of stale wine, sweat and sawdust. This was definitely not a place catering to the tourist market. In fact, it almost felt as though they'd trespassed into someone's private home. Suspicious eyes followed them as they made their way to the bar, and Lucius was grateful for the pugio, tucked discreetly in the belt of his tunic.

'Is Complexus Ursi here?' Isi asked the man at the bar. The dark-complexioned barman had long, silky brown hair and a neat beard. A gold chain dangled around his neck, to match the gold hoop in his ear. He finished polishing the horn goblet he was holding before raising his eyes to her.

'Who wants to know?'

'We're friends of Hierax,' said Isi, 'lanista of the Swords of Isis.'

The barman's mouth swelled into a surprisingly charming grin. 'Hierax, you say! We-ell, in that case, I don't mind telling you that I am the one you seek.' He took a deep bow. 'Complexus Ursi at your service. So how is the old scoundrel? I do hope he finds time to drop by while you folks are in town. He eyed the two of them more closely. 'You're a pair of strapping young fighters, aren't you? I see Hierax still has an eye for talent.'

Lucius glanced at Isi and a brief smile passed between them. Dressed in a loose-fitting tunic and showing off her muscular shoulders, Isi had deliberately made herself appear like a boy. Back on the ship, she had warned Lucius that she would assume the identity of Tycho as soon as they stepped ashore. It was something she always did, on Hierax's advice. If she dressed as a girl, and was then recognised by some local who had seen her in the arena, it could cause no end of trouble – maybe even disqualification from the tournament.

'Now! What can I get you kids to eat?' asked Ursus. 'Here, come sit down.'

Still grinning away, Ursus guided them to a vacant table and served them each a portion of what he called the 'local delicacy': hot barley gruel with mountain herbs and grated goats' cheese. Lucius found it surprisingly tasty, especially after twelve days of salted beef and dried vegetables.

Ursus came and joined them, clasping his hands and clinking his beringed fingers together. 'So, what can I do for you folks? Has Hierax sent you here to get the low-down on the opposition? I can tell you now there are some fine young fighters in town from Pergamum...'

'Actually,' interrupted Lucius, 'we're here about something else. Have you heard of someone called Galerius Horatius Canio?'

Ursus's smile vanished. He looked up sharply, screwed up his eyes, twitched his nose, and turned his head smartly one way, then the other. His quick movements reminded Lucius of some of the smarter rats on board the *Concordia*. He leaned in very close, so they could smell his breath – a blend of wine, honey and spices. 'Be very careful,' he said in a low, scary voice, 'before you go mentioning that name. That name is *hot* in this city right now.' He glanced over at his other customers, who had gone back to their muttered conversations. 'Come with me,' he said to Lucius and Isi, and they followed him through a door into a storeroom filled with amphorae* of wine. He motioned for them to sit on some stools gathered around a rough table. A pair of dice lay on the table, and Lucius guessed that the room doubled as a gambling den.

Ursus didn't sit, but paced the floor nervously in

* *amphorae: pottery jars with pointed ends.*

front of them. 'The powers-that-be in Rome have got wind that Canio is in Ephesus,' he said. 'They've sent legionary cohorts down here to scour the place, house to house. Heavy stuff, y'know? I've even had them in here hassling me. They figured out I was a guy who knew stuff. Course I told them nothing, pleaded ignorance. I don't mind helping the local lawmen with their enquiries from time to time, but I draw the line at selling out my fellow citizens to these agents of Rome. And far as I'm concerned, Canio is a fellow citizen. I don't exactly know what he's done, but he's an Ephesian now, and we Ephesians look after our own, y'know what I'm saying?'

'Do you know where he is?' asked Lucius.

Ursus's eyes flickered with suspicion. 'Maybe I do, maybe I don't. How do I know this ain't some trick and you kids ain't spies working for the legionaries?' Isi and Lucius exchanged helpless glances, neither of them sure how to respond. Then Ursus's face cracked into a smile. 'Of course I'd know if you were spies. I have a sixth sense about that sort of thing. Still, I'm curious: what's your interest in the man?'

Isi started to speak, but Lucius cut in: 'He's an old friend of my father's. I knew him when he was living in Rome. I wanted to pay my respects.'

'And who might your father be, if you don't mind my asking?'

Lucius could see the confusion in the innkeeper's face. He was wondering how a lowly gladiator's father could be friends with a senator. 'He was a… a former slave of Senator Canio's,' he replied off the top of his head. 'Canio freed him and they became friends.'

Ursus gazed at Lucius, thinking hard, before seeming to make up his mind. 'You'll find him in the Jewish quarter – across the agora and through the Gate of Mazeus and Mithridates. He lives in a small apartment above Heraclitus the baker's, with a fellow named John, who's what they call a Christian. Have you heard of them?'

Lucius said he had.

'We've got a whole bunch of them here in Ephesus. Nice enough folk, but they do like to preach! One even tried to convert me once. I politely explained that the only god for me is Mercury, protector of messengers, thieves, tricksters and gamblers – basically anyone who ever needed to make a fast getaway. Anyway, the Christians are giving your man sanctuary. You'll need to give the baker man a password to get to him. The current one, so I'm told, is *Ichthys*.'*

Beyond the Gate of Mazeus and Mithridates, they entered a warren of narrow, winding streets, lined with every kind of shop, including blacksmiths, barbers, jewellers, pharmacists, shoemakers, stone-cutters,

---

* Ichthys: *Greek for 'fish' – but also a secret Christian symbol, because the letters stand for 'Jesus Christ, Son of God, Saviour' in Greek.*

lampmakers and locksmiths. The air was heavy with the stench of freshly butchered animals and of urine from the fulleries,* which mingled oddly with the sweet, pungent scents of perfume makers and florists. They passed bookshops with windows piled high with scrolls, and stood aside for merchants on camels bearing baskets overflowing with spices. They stared at stalls displaying fabrics of unbelievable colour and complexity, and from all around them came a babble of competing sounds: dogs barking; elderly bearded men chanting with their heads buried in scrolls; stallholders raucously yelling out their bargains; women in headscarves arguing over the price of fruit; and preachers standing on upturned food crates with the light of certainty in their eyes, beseeching people to listen to them.

Finally, after several enquiries they arrived at the shop of Heraclitus the baker. Lucius felt his heart thudding in his chest as they entered the shop. Would they really find Canio here, and what news would the senator have for them?

Heraclitus was a big, fleshy man with a prominent nose, ruddy cheeks and a friendly smile. His freshly baked wares were displayed attractively on a stone counter in front of him: loaves and flatbreads of barley and wheat – some plain, others mixed with cheese or honey.

---

* *fulleries: laundries. Roman fullers used stale urine to clean and bleach cloth.*

He spoke some welcoming words in Greek, to which Isi responded fluently. When Lucius heard her mention the name Canio, Heraclitus's features furrowed into a worried frown. Nervously, he touched a silver cross dangling from a chain around his neck. Then Isi said the word *Ichthys*, and the baker nodded, seemingly satisfied. He beckoned them through a curtained entrance behind the counter and pointed up a narrow, twisting staircase.

Isi took the lead up the stairs. At the top lay a small landing, and she knocked on the only door. It was opened by a thin man in a cloak, with a long, ageless-seeming face. He had a grey beard, protruding cheekbones and dark eyes that impressed Lucius with their sadness and their strength. *This man has suffered loss*, Lucius thought, *yet he doesn't seem broken by it.*

Isi spoke to him in Greek, and she repeated the password. The man nodded, then raised his hand and made the sign of the cross in the air, first before Isi and then Lucius, muttering as he did so. Opening the door wider, he stood aside for them to enter.

The room was as bare as a cell, with two mattresses on the floor. Beneath the only window was a desk on which lay several papyrus scrolls, together with a reed pen and a bottle of ink. The wall to their right contained a niche where candles and incense burned. Carved into the wall at the back of this little shrine were the symbols of a fish and a cross, and other shapes and letters that Lucius did not recognise.

The man uttered a few short words, and a figure emerged from behind a shabby curtain covering a doorway on the left. It took Lucius a moment to recognise him.

'Senator Canio!' he cried.

Canio looked up, and Lucius was shocked by the transformation in him. The fat, cheerful, race-loving senator was no more. In his place was a gaunt, haggard man with hollow cheeks, heavy jowls and fearful eyes. His toga had been swapped for a rough tunic, and around his neck hung a simple wooden cross.

Recognition flooded Canio's face, and his eyes filled with tears as he embraced Lucius. 'Why, it's Aquila's boy,' he gasped. 'This is a miracle! I thought you were dead.'

Lucius hugged him back, his mind whirling with memories of that happy, sunny day at the race track a lifetime ago when they'd last met. But the senator he remembered had shrunk to little more than skin and bone – he could feel the old man's ribs protruding beneath the tunic.

'I heard that you'd drowned in the Pontine Marshes,' said Canio.

'As you can see, I survived,' said Lucius. 'But please tell me, sir, what news is there of my family?' He was almost frightened to hear Canio's reply.

'But surely you know about your father and brother...' said Canio, turning pale.

Lucius nodded, and as he did so, he felt something

sicken and die inside him. He realised it was hope – a feeble, flickering flame he must have been carrying inside him all these months – the hope that Quin had somehow survived the attack on the causeway. But Canio's expression forced him to accept the harsher truth: Quin had been hacked down that day – butchered in cold blood.

'What about Valeria?' Lucius managed to ask.

'I've heard nothing,' said Canio. 'We can only pray that if you survived, then maybe she did, too.'

Lucius held the older man's frail, bony hands. 'Canio, you must tell me everything you know.'

'Of course.' He turned to his roommate and exchanged a few words in Greek.

The bearded man nodded and picked up a small food crate like the ones Lucius had seen being used by street preachers. Then he left the apartment.

Canio stared after him. 'Remarkable man, that John,' he muttered. 'You wouldn't know it but he's over eighty years old. Half a century ago, he was one of the disciples of Our Lord Jesus Christ. Now, when he's not out preaching in the agora, he's up here writing an account of Jesus's life and teachings.' A dreamlike expression entered Canio's eyes. Almost to himself, he added: 'Like me, he was forced to witness the murder of his god.' Then he lowered his eyes. 'I have since understood the error in my thinking: Titus has no more divinity than I have, and the entire Roman pantheon*

* Pantheon: all the Roman gods and goddesses together.

is a childish fantasy next to the power and glory of the one true God.'

Canio blinked and seemed to recollect himself. He noticed Isidora for the first time, and inclined his head politely towards her as Lucius introduced them. Lucius was impatient to hear what Canio had to say. He desperately hoped that the man could shed some light on the mysteries that had obsessed him for six long months. But Canio insisted on hearing Lucius's story first – how Lucius had survived the Pontine Marshes, and how he and Isi came to be in Ephesus. When Lucius had finished his tale, Canio sighed. 'I'm sorry for your suffering, young man, but happy that you're alive, and grateful that the Lord has seen fit that our paths should cross once again.'

Isi, who had been looking idly out of the window during Lucius's account, suddenly became distracted by something she could see below her on the street. 'Excuse me, both of you,' she said, heading swiftly for the door. 'I just have to go and check on something. I'll be back soon.'

Lucius watched her go, wondering what she could have seen. Then he turned back to Canio. 'Please tell me what you know, sir,' he implored him. 'Who killed Titus? Who killed my father? Why did the Praetorians come after us?'

'I can answer all your questions with a single word,' replied Canio, 'but it will profit you nothing.' His eyes had taken on that dreamy look once more.

'We Christians believe that Christ will shortly return to Earth, he will gather up his followers, and we will ascend to Heaven together. All of God's enemies will perish on that day, including the murderer of your father. Rather than waste your energies with thoughts of petty revenge, why not join us? Why not become one of the saved?' Canio smiled expectantly at Lucius.

Lucius looked away. He found it hard to think clearly while held captive by Canio's calm, persuasive gaze. 'I'm sorry, sir,' he said. 'I respect your beliefs, but that is your path, not mine.'

He felt Canio's hand gently touch his shoulder. 'It's all right, my boy. But if you ever change your mind, we're here for you. We want to try and save as many as we can before the world comes to an end, you understand.'

Lucius clenched his fists to ease the tension in his stomach. When would the man tell him what he knew?

'You said just now that a single word would answer all my questions. What word is that?'

Canio turned away from him, and Lucius could see that the former senator's hands were shaking. He began to fear that he would get no further information out of him. Canio was staring longingly towards the little shrine in the wall as if trying to draw strength from it. Through trembling lips, he finally spoke the word that had been weighing on him:

'Glabrio.'

Glabrio? Lucius's mind raced. Marcus Acilius

Glabrio was a current Consul of Rome, and the host and protector of his mother – the man whose house they'd been trying to get to when they were ambushed by the Praetorians.

'What about him?' Lucius asked.

Canio continued to focus on the shrine. When he spoke again, his voice was empty of feeling: 'Glabrio killed Titus. He also killed your father – or at least ordered his death. And he gave the order to the Praetorians to kill or capture you and your brother and sister.'

Lucius shook his head firmly. 'No, you're mistaken. Glabrio tried to protect us. My mother wanted to take us to his house on the night of Father's murder – she said he'd keep us safe. And then the next morning, after the murder, he again offered us his protection against further attacks. He even sent us an escort to take us to his house. We were on our way there when the Praetorians captured us.'

Canio was trembling all over now. He turned on Lucius almost angrily: 'And did you ever think, boy, how the Praetorians knew you would be passing that particular empty shop at that particular time? Who could have told them that except Glabrio?'

Lucius's head was spinning. This couldn't possibly be right, could it? 'But his own personal attendant, Ennius, was killed in the ambush!'

Canio merely shrugged. 'The consul deliberately sacrificed the boy to make himself appear innocent.'

'Why would he do that? Why would he bother to appear innocent to us, if we were going to die anyway?'

'It wasn't you he was concerned about – it was your mother,' Canio said bitterly. 'He wanted her to believe that someone else was responsible for her children's deaths.'

Lucius tried to get his breathing under control. This was all too much to take in. 'OK… you'll have to start from the beginning, sir. How do you know Glabrio killed Titus?'

'Your father and I discovered it during our visit to Aquae Cutiliae.'

'He was the person you followed?'

Canio nodded.

'And he was the one who forced the cook to poison the sea-hare?'

'Correct.'

'But why would he want to kill the emperor? He was consul! He'd done well under Titus, hadn't he?'

'Being consul isn't much use to someone as ambitious as Glabrio, unless you have influence with the emperor,' said Canio with a sour laugh. 'But Glabrio and Titus were barely on speaking terms. You see, Glabrio could never forgive Titus for destroying his best friend – your uncle, Ravilla.'

'So why did Titus make him consul?'

'Titus always liked to keep his enemies close. He hoped it would stop them plotting. It was his worst mistake. Glabrio was, and still is, close to Titus's brother Domitian, and he knew he'd have more power under Domitian, so it was in his interests for Titus to die. I'm sure he'd been planning the assassination for quite some time, he just needed an opportunity.'

'How can you be sure he also killed my father?'

'It's obvious, isn't it? Think about the timing. He must have discovered somehow that Aquila was about to reveal all to the Senate, so he had to silence him fast. Glabrio also had a long-standing grievance against your father for his role in bringing down Ravilla, so he probably saw it as an act of revenge.'

Lucius knew then that Canio was right: Glabrio was his enemy. It sickened him to think of his mother living under the same roof as that monster. It was Lucius's ill luck that his nemesis was one of the most powerful men in Rome. That wouldn't stop Lucius, though: he would find a way to get to him...

'Once I'd heard that your father had been killed, I knew my days were numbered,' said Canio, gnawing at a loose thumbnail. 'If Glabrio knew about Aquila, he had to know about me as well. I tried to escape from Rome, but was captured. I happened to share my cell with a Christian named Cletus. His friends managed to spring us both from prison and bring us to Ephesus. The Christian community here have been very kind. At great risk to themselves, they've sheltered me, moving me from house to house so that I'm always one step ahead of my pursuers... But I know I'll never be safe. Glabrio has the emperor's ear, and the full might of imperial authority behind him in his quest to hunt me down.' He smiled tightly. 'He can only ever kill my body, though. My soul belongs to Christ.'

There was a knock on the door, and Canio visibly flinched – perhaps he wasn't quite so unconcerned about threats to his body as he claimed.

Lucius opened it to find Isi standing there looking breathless.

'Where have you been?' he asked her.

'I saw a hooded figure staring up at us from the street just now,' panted Isi. 'I thought I saw the same figure earlier in the agora... I ran after him, but lost him down some alleyway.'

Canio went back to chewing his thumbnail. 'You were followed, then,' he muttered. 'That means they've discovered me. I'll tell John when he gets back. They'll have to move me to another lodging tonight.'

'We'd better go,' said Lucius. 'Thank you, sir, for everything you've told me. I hope you manage to stay safe.'

Canio clasped Lucius's hands and held them tightly. 'I understand your desire for revenge, young man, but you must try to let it go. We have no power against men like that – not in this world. If you go up against Glabrio, he will crush you like an insect... It's not up to us to punish people anyway; that's God's work. Fear not: Glabrio will be punished.'

CHAPTER X

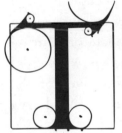he swords clashed so hard, sparks flew. Time and again, the big Murmillo came at Lucius, striking towards his helmet, his chest, his legs, forcing him to parry and making his forearms ache from the shockwaves of the repeated blows.

But Lucius was fighting within himself. Thanks to his work with Hierax, he was mastering the arts of patience, timing and observation. As the trainer often told him: you can learn far more about your opponent when he is attacking you. So Lucius observed the style and rhythm of the Murmillo, scenting hints of weakness in his footwork, in the positioning of his shield, in the tightness of his grip. All this would be useful knowledge when Lucius went on the offensive.

He could hear the man's grunting breath inside his helmet – a telltale sign that he was getting tired, as well as frustrated that he couldn't land a blow. A particularly vicious chop landed on the edge of Lucius's shield with such force that it nearly dislocated his arm. Lucius forced himself to be patient just a little longer – to weather the storm and wait for the mistakes creep in, as they were bound to eventually.

They were fighting in the D-shaped arena of the Theatre of Ephesus. On one side rose a steep, high bank of semicircular seating, carved into the green slope of Mount Pion, with its twin camel humps. As Hierax had predicted, the seats were packed to capacity, and the noise the crowd was making was even louder than that generated by the Carthaginian spectators during his previous fight. Much more subdued were the chief priest of the Temple of Artemis – the giver of the games – and his entourage, seated in the central area near the front.

The Murmillo continued to hack away at Lucius, driving him slowly back towards the skene, a three-storeyed edifice ornamented with columns, relief carvings and statues that stood at the back of the stage, opposite the spectators' seating. This building was normally used to store theatrical props and as a place for actors to change costumes during dramatic performances. For these gladiatorial games, however, it served as a waiting area for the fighters and an armoury. In front of the building stood a line of iron-barred cages occupied by the wild animals used during the morning beast hunts. It was towards these that the Murmillo seemed determined to push Lucius. As he was pressed nearer to them, Lucius could hear excited snufflings and stampings of hoofs and – most worryingly – the guttural roar of a large lion.

This was not how things were supposed to go. The Murmillo was proving a stubborn old devil, refusing to relent in his attacks, despite sounding close to exhaustion, and offering no obvious opportunities for counterattack. Lucius could sense the hunger and agitation of the animals to his rear. If the Murmillo forced him against the bars of any of those cages, his back might be gored or ripped to shreds by tusks, teeth or claws.

Lucius knew that he had to find a way of breaking up his adversary's rhythm – but how? There was only one way, and he knew it. He would have to do as Hierax and Isi had advised, and try to hate this man. As he blocked and parried each dogged sword strike, he found time to glance up at the crested helmet and the monstrous grille that covered the face of the Murmillo. He pictured the red, sweating face inside there, and he imagined it transformed into something cooler and paler – a narrow face with hooded eyes and a hooked nose – the face, so far as he remembered it, of Consul Marcus Acilius Glabrio.

As the image completed itself in his mind, cool hatred bled into his heart, and Lucius was surprised at the pleasure that accompanied it, and the extra energy it seemed to stir within his aching muscles. At the very next strike towards his shoulder, he didn't just block, he shoved forward. The gladiators' swords became locked at the hilt as both pressed hard against each other. Lucius could smell the man's warm, garlicky breath, mingling with the reek of beast sweat behind him. The animals, he knew, were very close now. He could feel their spittle spraying his shoulders. A mental picture came to him of Glabrio giving the order to kill his father, and he drove a hard punch into the man's unprotected flank.

The Murmillo staggered back in surprise, and Lucius siezed his chance. With a strength and speed that surprised even him, he unleashed his anger, raining down sword blows from left, right and above. It was like his fight with Hierax on the deck of the *Concordia* when he'd first discovered the means of channelling this inner rage – only this time he'd done it without any help from his opponent. As happened then, he felt somehow detached, yet right at the centre of the action, as if his body was a chariot and he was the driver. Pain flooded his muscles, yet he drove himself on – the ice-burn of hatred in his heart slaying all the doubts, all the flaking of nerves and will that might once have made him frail.

The crowd went quiet for a few moments as they absorbed this sudden reversal in the momentum of the fight. Then the cheers – fickle cheers – started up again, even louder than before, in support of their new favourite: the unknown young Hoplomachus, Alecto. As for the poor Murmillo, he was forced into a blind, stumbling retreat, fending off the blows as best he could, bleeding from a wound to his arm, foiled at every attempted counterstrike. The end came quickly, with the Murmillo slipping on some blood from a previous fight and falling directly beneath the marble seat of the high priest of Artemis, Lucius's swordpoint at his throat.

'Apeluthe!' came the cries. 'Apokteinon!'

The demands for death were much louder than those for mercy, but the high priest – perhaps worrying about the cost of reimbursing a lanista for a dead gladiator – offered the shielded thumb. Lucius helped the defeated Murmillo to his feet, heartily relieved at the decision. The moment his adversary had hit the dust, all the hatred had drained out of him. Now the physical toll of the fight struck: he felt exhausted and in pain throughout most of his body, and the elation he'd expected to feel after his first victory wasn't there. Instead, he felt hollowed out, as if the inner hatred he'd let loose to give him victory had taken something from him in return.

He held his sword up in a triumphant salute to the cheering crowd, trying to suck in some of their joy to fill the emptiness inside him. He spotted attendants moving along the aisles with silver collecting trays, and was relieved to see spectators tossing handfuls of coins into them. At last he would be able to repay Hierax something for his faith in him. He'd already decided he wouldn't be joining the Swords on their trip to Corinth, so the more he could earn for this fight, the better. He was going to head back to Rome on the next available boat to carry out his mission of vengeance and kill Consul Glabrio. He'd told Isi what he'd learned from Canio, but hadn't mentioned his plan of revenge. He hoped she would understand that he had to return to Rome.

As these thoughts flashed through his mind, he suddenly noticed that the cheering around him had died, replaced by a collective gasp and shudder. He saw wide-eyed shock on the faces in the crowd – even the normally impassive priests looked startled, and he wondered what they could see. Then, from just behind him, there came a deep, threatening growl, full of savagery and hunger, and he went limp with fear.

The lion! It must have escaped its cage!

The creature, when he turned to face it, seemed out of proportion: huge head, jaws and humped shoulders, tapering away to a normal-sized body and tail. To his left, the wounded Murmillo looked terrified as he slowly edged his way around the perimeter wall towards the exit. Lucius was vaguely aware of a team of slaves armed with spears being reluctantly forced into the arena. But they were far away, and the lion was close, and getting closer. Its yellow eyes were narrowed on Lucius, and when it opened its jaws and he saw the array of vicious, dagger-like teeth, he wanted to scream.

A movement by the Murmillo, or perhaps the smell of his bleeding arm, diverted the lion's attention, and suddenly its ravenous gaze was fixed on him. It growled menacingly. The Murmillo tried to run, but stumbled over his feet. The lion leapt. The gladiator screamed. Lucius swung his sword at the lion, but the blade simply bounced off the thick, matted mane. Another scream split the air, and a red torrent spurted across the sand. The crowd groaned. Lucius could barely look at the mess of blood and bone that had been his opponent. As the lion fed, he plunged his sword into its side. The beast roared in pain. Lucius tried to withdraw his sword, but it got stuck in the ribs and as the lion turned on him, he lost his grip on the hilt. It sprang at him, its blood-drenched claws and teeth bared. Lucius, who'd dropped his shield earlier, fell to his knees and raised his arms in a vain attempt to protect his head.

The lion never reached him. A spear pierced it through the neck, and it fell, dead, within a foot of where Lucius knelt. He stared disbelievingly at the creature that had come so close to killing him. Its eyes and mouth now closed, it seemed to have shrunk to little more than an oversized, sleeping cat. Only the blood around its mouth was a reminder of what it had been. Lucius reached out and touched its dark mane – still warm, and surprisingly soft. He looked up to see Isi standing there – breathless, distressed, but also hugely relieved.

'I picked up a spear and ran out of the skene,' she cried. 'I didn't have much time to aim – I just threw it.' She fell to the ground and hugged him. 'Oh, Lucius... We nearly lost you!'

The audience cheered, clearly appreciating this demonstration of friendship between two gladiators – a breed not normally known for such displays.

'Your aim was good,' said Lucius. 'It must be all that time spent skewering rats on the *Concordia*.'

'That's the biggest rat I ever skewered,' said Isi, smiling through her tears.

'Well, I owe you my life,' said Lucius. 'Thank you.'

She sniffed and wiped her eyes. 'Just before it happened, I saw that hooded fellow again, over by the animal cages.'

Lucius stared at her.

As slaves hauled away the carcasses of the lion and the Murmillo, leaving great smears of blood through the sand, Lucius and Isi headed over to the lion's cage. A cluster of concerned-looking officials had gathered there, pointing at the open cage door and remonstrating with each other in angry Greek.

'They're accusing each other of failing to secure the cage,' translated Isi. Then her eye fell on something on the ground – a wooden mallet. She picked it up, and looked again at the cage door. 'This must have been used by someone to knock out the wooden peg that holds the door closed...' Her eyes widened, and she grabbed Lucius's arm in a fierce grip. 'It was the man in the hood! While everyone was watching you win your fight, he must have crept over here and knocked out the peg.'

Lucius felt his mouth go dry.

'He tried to kill me...'

Lucius remained in the skene for the rest of the afternoon, watching his fellow Swords fight their bouts. He was pleased and relieved to see each of them emerge victorious and relatively unscathed. Isi, or rather Tycho, defeated a much bigger Hoplomachus by hooking her curved sword around his shield and striking at his exposed chest.

But, except when his friends were involved, Lucius found it hard to concentrate on the action in the arena. He kept looking around him, his hand never more than an inch from the dagger in his belt, hoping to spot the mysterious hooded assassin before he was leapt on and killed. Could it be the same man that Isi had seen yesterday outside Canio's apartment? Could it even be the same one who killed his father? No, surely not.

But what if it was?

What if this faceless figure was an agent of Glabrio's? If so, he might be capable of almost anything. Like a ghost, he seemed to be able to scale high walls and evade guards, disappear down alleyways and unbolt a lion's cage in full view of 25,000 people. He could strike anywhere at any time. It made Lucius even more determined to part company with the Swords as soon as possible. If he was being stalked by this killer, then travelling with a group of colourful characters could make him conspicuous. He might be safer on his own.

As Lucius and his fellow Swords were leaving the theatre to head back to their barracks at the local ludus, they were intercepted by a mob of fans who broke through the roped walkway down which the gladiators were being guided. An irate theatre official yelled at the fans in Greek and tried to interpose himself between them and their heroes.

Hierax broke free of a fan's embrace and pointed at the ludus, which was only twenty or thirty paces away. 'Quick, let's run for it!' he yelled.

Lucius tried to run with the others, but he was held back by a hand that clamped itself to his arm. Exasperated, he tried to free himself, but was stayed by a familiar voice.

'My man! Alecto, ain't it?'

The man holding him was none other than Complexus Ursi, the bar owner they'd met yesterday. He'd shouldered his way to the front of the throng and was now getting jostled by those behind.

'Hey, let go, you scoundrels,' he bellowed at them. 'This is a high-quality tunic I'm wearing!'

'Hello, Ursus!' shouted Lucius. 'You should come over to the ludus. I'm sure Hierax would be glad to see you.'

'Can't stay, I'm afraid, kid. Got some business needs seeing to.' The smile of yesterday was missing from Ursus's face. 'Just came by to give you the news – sad news – about your man Canio.'

Ursus's grip on Lucius slipped as fans got between them and tried to hoist Lucius onto their shoulders.

Lucius wrestled himself free of them. 'What happened?' he called.

'He was killed,' Ursus yelled back. 'His body was found this morning in an alleyway.' Before he could say more, Ursus got caught up in a stream of human traffic and he was carried away.

Lucius stared back at the retreating figure, stunned. He wanted to ask more questions, but Ursus had disappeared from view.

'I have to leave,' Lucius said to Isi, as soon as he'd managed to get back to the ludus.

'What?' cried Isi. 'Aren't you coming to Corinth with us? We'll be leaving in a couple of days.'

'Canio's dead.'

Isi's hand went to her mouth.

'If I stay here one more day, I'll be killed too, I'm sure of it. You saw what happened with the lion. That man in the hood – he must be Glabrio's agent.'

'Then I'm in just as much danger as you,' said Isi. 'Why?'

'Because he saw both of us go into Canio's apartment. That must be why you've been targeted.'

'No,' said Lucius. 'You've got it the wrong way round. Glabrio's agent couldn't have known that was Canio's apartment – or else Canio would have been dead long ago. It's obvious what happened: I was recognised; I led him there.' He hung his head as the implications sank in. 'Canio is dead because of me.'

He felt Isi's sympathetic hand on his shoulder. 'You can't blame yourself.'

'I must go to Rome,' said Lucius, not looking up. 'Why?'

He didn't want to admit his plan to kill Glabrio – didn't want to be told by her how ludicrous it was. 'Because I need to warn my mother about the man whose house she's living in… and I want to find out what happened to my sister.'

'We should go and talk to Hierax,' said Isi.

They found the lanista coming out of the dormitory in his loincloth, with a towel slung over his shoulder. 'Can this wait?' he said. 'I'm just heading over to the bath-house for a wash and massage before dinner.'

Isi came straight to the point: 'We can't join you in Corinth.'

Lucius was startled by this – though Hierax seemed less so.

'Wait a minute, it's me who's not going, not both of us,' Lucius objected.

Isi shook her head. 'I'm coming with you,' she said firmly. Turning back to Hierax, she explained: 'Lucius and I are going to Rome.'

Again, Lucius found himself amazed. He never thought he'd hear her say those words. Rome had been the city of her enslavement. Why would she ever want to return there?

Hierax merely nodded. The only emotion his scarred face seemed to register was regret. 'Isidora, I told you when you joined up that you were free to leave at any time. That's the founding principle of the Swords of Isis – we're freeborn fighters, with the power to choose our own destinies... I wish you both success in Rome. And I hope you'll see fit to rejoin us when you've completed your business there. By the way, I thought you were magnificent today, Lucius. You did us all proud.'

Lucius didn't sleep at all that night. He lay on his bed, one hand resting on his dagger hilt, watching and waiting for an attack. He'd tried to dissuade Isi from coming with him to Rome, worrying that he'd be more conspicious travelling with her. But Isi had insisted. 'I'm just as involved in this as you are,' she'd argued. 'Glabrio's agent will assume you've told me everything, so I'm now also a target. Anyway, together we'll be stronger. Four eyes are better than two. We can protect each other!' In the end, Lucius had agreed, secretly pleased to have her company.

No attack came that night. The pair rose early and made their way to the harbour of Ephesus. Within an hour, they had negotiated a berth on the Rome-bound merchant ship, the *Cygnus*.* Not willing to spend their money on a cabin, they decided to take deck passage. As the crewmen finished loading up the ship's cargo of goat-hair cloth, silks and spices, Lucius and Isi visited some quayside shops to stock up on provisions for the journey, some blankets and a collapsible canvas shelter. Lucius remained tense the whole time they were on shore, and was only able to start to relax once they had cleared the harbour and entered the open sea.

They shared a breakfast of bread, cheese and raisins while sitting beneath their deck shelter, watching the mountainous island of Samos slide past them.

'I still can't believe you're coming back to Rome,' remarked Lucius.

'Nor can I,' admitted Isi. 'But I really couldn't let

---

* Cygnus: *swan. Roman merchant ships traditionally had a carving of a swan at the stern.*

you go alone. You'll need someone to watch your back.'
She gave him a sidelong glance. 'I'm guessing the real
reason why you're going there is to kill Glabrio, right?'

So she'd guessed! Lucius gave a wry smile and
nodded.

'You're a fool,' said Isi. 'You know it's impossible.
People like that don't go anywhere without an army of
lictors* surrounding them. You'd be cut down before
you could get within ten paces of him.'

Lucius shrugged and chewed on his bread.

'You've got a death wish as strong as Quin ever
had, you know that?' Isi persisted.

She didn't understand! Lucius tried to explain
his thinking. 'When I was lying at the bottom of that
swamp, I made a choice to go on living,' he said, 'but
only so that I could avenge the murders of my father
and brother. That's all I live for now. Nothing else.
You can call it a death wish, if you like, but that's the
way it is.'

'You've changed,' murmured Isi. 'You're not the
boy I knew.'

Lucius nodded. 'I don't feel like a boy any more.
I feel more like a… like a weapon… a weapon with a
single purpose: vengeance. It's my destiny, I'm sure of
it. Everything that's happened to me – getting captured
by that slave dealer, being trained as a gladiator, being
taught by Hierax – it's all been to strengthen me, to
prepare me for this one task.'

* *lictors: official bodyguards.*

'To kill Glabrio? And will that make things better? It won't bring your father or brother back.'

'I know, but... there are other things at stake here. Glabrio is determined to wipe out my family – not just its members, but also its name. He's trying to portray my father as a traitor. He wants to blacken the name of the Valerii.'

'How do you know that?'

'The Praetorian officer who captured us, Scaro – I'm sure he's Glabrio's puppet – anyway, he called me "spawn of a snake". Another one called me "son of a traitor". Glabrio must be spreading the lie that my father is a traitor, and I have to stop him. I also have to stop him from stealing my property.'

'Property!' said Isi scornfully. 'Is that what this is all about, then?'

Lucius flashed her an angry look. 'Land means everything to a Roman. I don't expect you to understand, but that house on the Esquiline has belonged to my family for centuries. Its soil is part of who I am – as are the household gods in the atrium shrine. My ancestors were buried there, and their wax masks line the walls in the tablinum. That house belongs to me! But Glabrio will marry my mother, I'm sure of it, just so he can get hold of that property. He doesn't need it, but it'll be another way of humiliating my family.'

Lucius surprised himself with his own anger and misery, as these long-repressed thoughts bubbled up into words. He felt Isi's hand in his, and held on to it tightly.

'I understand humiliation,' she said quietly. 'Your people did that to me and my family. Whatever you decide to do, I'll be here for you.'

He felt a sob start to build in his throat and gritted his teeth until it went away. He didn't want to cry. He wanted to be cold and ruthless, like a weapon.

Three days later, the *Cygnus* arrived at the port of Chersonasos in Crete. Lucius and Isi leaned on the ship's rail and observed the hundreds of small boats bobbing in the bright blue waters. Fishermen held aloft huge, still-writhing silver fish and shouted prices up at them. Isi laughed and shook her head. The merchant captain had assured them that they would get much better bargains on shore.

The crew tossed ropes to the dockers and used the steering oars to guide the ship safely into the quayside. Lucius and Isi were eager to stretch their legs, and as soon as the gangplank was lowered, they took off into the town. By the time they returned in the early afternoon, the ship had been loaded up with its additional cargo of olive oil – and a new passenger had come on board.

The young man was standing on the deck when they arrived, with his back to them, looking out to sea. He turned as they approached, and his face lit up. 'Hello!' he called cheerfully. 'You must be my fellow passengers. I'm... er...' His voice tailed away. 'Why, don't I know you, sir?' he said, squinting at Lucius.

Lucius studied the youth's round, handsome face, framed by dark curls, and a shiver of recognition ran through him. His voice, with its clipped, well-educated accent, was also familiar. He did know this person, he just couldn't place him. 'What's your name?' he asked.

'Eprius Domitius Piso – but please call me Eprius. And you, sir, if I'm not mistaken, are... Wait a minute. I've got it! You're Lucius, aren't you?'

'Gods!' cried Lucius, as the memories returned in a rush. 'Of course I remember you, Eprius. How could I forget our adventure in Pompeii? How are you? You look so... different.'

Eprius had been a rather pale and delicate-looking boy when Lucius last saw him nearly three years ago. Now he'd grown taller, and his slender limbs were well toned with muscle, his chest had broadened and his skin had darkened. The transformation was, if anything, even more dramatic than Lucius's own.

'As do you, my good fellow!' cried Eprius, clasping Lucius's arm in friendship. 'That must be why I had trouble placing you at first.'

'The body you see is the result of my misfortunes,' explained Lucius. 'My father and brother were killed. I was forced into slavery and sold to a gladiator school. Now I'm on my way back to Rome to search for my sister.' He dropped his voice to a whisper: 'And, by the way, I'm Alecto – no longer Lucius.'

Eprius nodded solemnly. 'Alecto... I will remember. I'm so sorry for your loss. I saw your brother fight in Pompeii, do you remember? He was magnificent.' His glance fell on Isi and he gave a bow. 'To whom do I owe the pleasure?'

Isi giggled at his high-class manners. 'I'm Isidora,' she said. 'Sometimes I'm a girl, sometimes a boy.'

Eprius looked confused.

'She's a gladiator, like me,' explained Lucius. 'She fights under the name Tycho.'

'That makes three of us,' laughed Eprius.

'You, too?' gaped Lucius.

'I'm a Murmillo – for my sins.'

'Mortal enemy!' cried Isi in mock horror. She showed him her fist with index and little fingers extended as if to ward off evil. 'I'm a Thraex, and Lucius is a Hoplomachus.'

'Well, then I sincerely hope we never have to cross swords in an arena,' said Eprius tactfully.

'You have to tell me your story,' said Lucius. 'How did you come to be a gladiator?'

In truth, Lucius felt a little guilty about his treatment of Eprius. After they had escaped the eruption of Vesuvius, he had taken him back to Rome, but had more or less abandoned him after that. Eprius's entire family had been wiped out by the eruption, so he would have had no one to turn to. Lucius would probably have helped him in normal times, but he'd been so focused on nursing his brother back to health, and worrying about his father, that he'd forgotten about his friend from Pompeii.

But if Eprius had been hurt by Lucius's treatment of him, he didn't show it now. 'I decided to go travelling,' he said amiably, 'and I fetched up here in Crete, where I joined the gladiator school at Gortyn. To be frank, I was penniless by this time and needed the money. But it turned out I had a flair for the fighting arts. I seemed to win every bout. I'm sure my ancestors were looking down on me in grave disapproval – it's not the life for a young nobleman – but it seemed to come naturally to me. After two and a half years, I've become primus palus* at the ludus, and made a stack of money. Now I aim to try my luck in Rome.'

'You don't like Crete, then?' asked Isi.

'Oh, it's very nice and all, but a bit of a backwater, and not exactly challenging for a young gladiator. In fact, they say the last exciting fight on this island was Theseus versus the Minotaur.'**

They all laughed.

Eprius eyed the deck shelter Lucius and Isi were sharing. 'I say, do you two fancy an upgrade? How

* *primus palus: top fighter (literally 'first post', referring to the wooden posts used as targets for sword practice).*

** *Theseus versus the Minotaur: in Greek legend, the Minotaur was a monster, part man, part bull, kept in an underground maze (the Labyrinth) on Crete. The Greek hero Theseus killed it with the help of the Cretan princess Ariadne. Eprius is joking that nothing exciting has happened on Crete for centuries.*

about I get you the cabin next door to mine? My treat.'

Isi and Lucius swapped a look. 'Thanks, Eprius,' said Lucius, 'but the nights are mild, and we're happy up here under the stars. Of course, if the weather turns between here and Rome, we may take you up on your kind offer.'

'Of course – just let me know.'

Isi said something to Eprius in Greek, to which he replied, and they began to converse. Lucius watched them contentedly as they jabbered away. He'd forgotten much of his Greek, and could barely follow what they were saying. But he was so happy to have chanced upon his old friend, and relieved he didn't bear him any ill-will. The rest of the voyage promised to be fun.

The rest of the voyage would have been a lot more fun, but for Isi and her odd behaviour. Something seemed to have changed in her during the course of the twelve-day sea journey, and Lucius found her increasingly hard to deal with. She simply wouldn't leave his side. The ship wasn't exactly big, and Lucius sometimes felt the need for some privacy. Yet, if he ever took a stroll around the deck, Isi would always insist on coming with him. At night, as he lay next to her under their canvas shelter, he often had the feeling that she was keeping watch over him. It was very weird.

Sometimes, Lucius felt like spending time with Eprius. They had shared an amazing adventure in Pompeii, and would have enjoyed reminiscing about it, except that Isi was always there with them, which made the conversations awkward and stilted. Lucius would have liked to open up to Eprius about the real reason for their return to Rome. It had been Eprius, after all, who had helped him uncover the full extent of Ravilla's evil. They'd been partners back in Pompeii, spying on Valens and Ravilla and facing dangers together. He would really value Eprius's help now. But whenever he suggested the idea to Isi, she always vetoed it: 'The fewer people know, the safer we'll be.'

One afternoon, the three of them were relaxing on deck, watching the crewmen holding the two great steering oars steady against the current. One of the steerers gave a low whistle and before long an athletic-looking sailor leapt down from the rigging and sauntered over. The steerer pointed to something that had got caught in his oar – perhaps some seaweed or a fishing net. The sailor removed his cloth cap and tied a rope around his waist. Then, without a word, he dived off the back of the ship. The three passengers rushed to the stern to watch as he resurfaced. In a few powerful strokes he'd caught hold of the steering oar. Using his knife he quickly freed the oar of its encumbrance before being hauled back up on deck by his colleagues.

'That looks like fun,' declared Eprius. 'Do you fancy having a go?'

'Having a go at what, exactly?' queried Lucius. 'There's nothing entangling the oars now.'

Eprius had a brief dialogue in Greek with the dripping sailor, before turning back to Lucius. 'He says there are barnacles on the steering oars. How about we each have a go at scraping some of them off? The winner is the one who brings back most.'

Lucius looked over the side. It was a hot day, and the deep blue water looked so cool and inviting. 'OK,' he said. 'Let's do it.'

'No,' said Isi. 'Let's not do it.'

'Come on, Isi,' said Lucius. 'It's not like you to chicken out of a contest.'

'It's dangerous,' she said through tight lips. 'The sailor mentioned there are sometimes sharks here.'

'Oh yes, I didn't quite follow that part,' admitted Eprius. 'What's a shark?'

'A big fish with lots of teeth,' she snapped. 'It could eat you in two gulps.'

Lucius peered into the silky blue depths, suddenly not feeling quite so keen.

'Just stories, I'm sure,' insisted Eprius. 'There's nothing down there to harm us. Who wants to go first? Alecto?'

Perhaps it was to prove himself in front of the crewmen and Eprius, or perhaps it was to spite Isi, who was really getting on his nerves – Lucius wasn't exactly sure of the reason, but he immediately nodded his head. The sailor grinned, showing a few missing teeth, and handed him the tar-sealed end of the rope. Lucius tied it around his waist. The other end was secured to an iron bolt on the deck. Lucius stripped down to his loincloth and placed his knife between his teeth, since he had nowhere else to put it. Then he stepped onto the narrow wooden platform that ran around the stern and readied himself for the dive.

Isi called from behind: 'Don't do it – please!' – but that only made him more determined.

He looked down and gulped – he was a good twenty feet above the sea. He bent his knees, trying to remember the few dives he'd made on a long-ago visit to the Piscina Publica.* *Keep hands and feet together!* He took a deep breath and dived between the two oars.

Lucius hit the surface with a smack and plunged into the blue, which was much colder than he had expected. He felt a jerk as he reached the limit of the rope. When he surfaced, he found he had to swim hard just to keep up – the *Cygnus* was faster than it appeared when on deck. Using all his strength, he ploughed through the water until he was close enough to grab the end of the starboard oar. But his fingers slid off the slippery, seaweed-covered surface. As he sank, he took an involuntary gulp of salt water. He surfaced, choking and spluttering. The knife was forcing his mouth open, so he transferred it to his hand.

* *Piscina Publica: public swimming pool.*

A dark shadow seemed to dart just below the surface. A shark? He tried to close his mind to the horrifying possibility and focus instead on the oar in front of him. Three more times he clutched at it, and each time his hand slid off. He was reaching the limits of his energy. Cold was cramping his muscles. He was becoming helpless bait for the sharks.

The fourth time, though, he managed to hold on. As he tried to gain a better grip, more water got into his lungs, making him cough. Desperately, he tried to scrape off some barnacles, but now the rope was tautening. They were bringing him up.

'Hold on!' he cried, but they didn't hear him. Isi was screaming something, and pointing. He twisted around, and saw a grey fin knifing towards him through the blue water. As he was hauled upwards out of the sea, he heard a snapping sound close by and thought for a paralysing second that it was the rope breaking. Then he realised it was the snap of jaws. He was thankful never to have seen how close they were.

A minute later he was on his knees on deck, coughing and trying to regain his breath. When he managed to look up, it was to see Isi staring icily at Eprius.

'Satisfied?' she said to him.

'I'm sorry,' said Eprius palely. 'That was stupid of me.'

Lucius shook his head, and retched. 'Never mind,' he said. 'Take a look at this.'

He held out his hand. There were five little barnacles nestling in the centre of his palm.

PART THREE

SIGN OF THE KESTREL

CHAPTER XI

18 APRIL

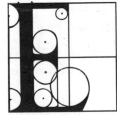prius was almost bouncing with excitement as he, Lucius and Isi walked east through the Campus Martius in Rome. Every few hundred paces they came upon another building or monument to provoke his gasps of awe: there was the gleaming marble curve of the Theatre of Pompey, rebuilt after the fire two years earlier; and the newly rising Stadium of Domitian; and the Diribitorium, where Rome's citizens went to cast their votes; and the great looping racetrack of the Circus Flaminius. Then there was the Baths of Agrippa, and the Pantheon, and… The sights went on and on.

While Eprius was busy gawping like a tourist, Lucius was anxiously scanning the scene for any

Praetorian guards. According to Canio, he was now officially dead, so no one would be out searching for him. Even so, the Campus Martius was a little too public for his liking, and there was always a chance he'd be recognised.

They reached the Saepta Julia market hall, and Eprius's attention was quickly captivated by the pretty displays of food, spices and luxury goods.

'By Jove!' he cried. 'I never saw treasures like these back in Gortyn!'

As he wandered over to the stalls, Isi raised her eyes in irritation. 'He's been like this ever since we got off the boat,' she whispered to Lucius. 'He's going to draw attention to us. We have to shake him off.'

'He doesn't know anyone in Rome,' Lucius reminded her. 'I can't just abandon him like I did last time – he was a good friend to me in Pompeii. How far is it to Faustina's?'

Earlier that day, before they left the ship, Isi had suggested that they head to the apartment of her friend Faustina, a former slave and co-worker at the Ludus Romanus. Both Faustina and Isidora had been freed by Aquila on his return from exile. Lucius hoped that Faustina would have news of Valeria.

'I'm not taking Eprius to Faustina's apartment,' asserted Isi.

'Why not?' asked Lucius, who had assumed that Isi had been including Eprius in their plans.

She glanced furtively at Eprius, who was at that

moment ogling a jewellery display of silver, gold and Baltic amber. 'He's too, well... loud! We can't trust him to keep our plans secret. Involving him will endanger us all.'

Lucius eyed his tall, wide-eyed, innocent friend. He couldn't desert him – not again! And who was to say he couldn't be trusted? If Lucius explained the nature of their plans, he was sure Eprius could be discreet.

'Either he comes with us, or I'm not going,' said Lucius firmly.

Isi snorted with frustration. 'OK,' she said sullenly. 'But I'll be keeping a very close eye on him.'

Faustina lived in an apartment in a six-storey insula on the Quirinal Hill, near the Temple of Flora. The stairwell stank uninvitingly of urine, charcoal and rancid oil. After a steep, twisting climb to the fifth floor, they knocked on her door. It opened almost immediately.

Faustina laughed when she saw Isi, and they embraced. 'Isi, what a fantastic surprise!' She pulled away. 'Gods! Look at you!' she cried, taking in Isi's slender body, muscular shoulders and deep brown skin. 'You look fantastic! Like Bellona!* I feel like a fat, middle-aged matron next to you.'

'What rubbish,' cried Isi. 'You're as beautiful as ever.'

---

* *Bellona: the Roman goddess of war.*

Faustina was about the same age as Isi, but very different-looking, with milky skin and plump, rounded features. When she saw Lucius, she clamped her hands to her cheeks and almost screamed in shock. 'Lucius, I thought you were dead!'

'And it's good to see you, too,' smiled Lucius.

'I'm sorry,' she blushed, 'but I just can't believe my eyes. Your death was announced. You even have a stone marker in the city cemetery.' Hesitantly, she reached out and touched him. 'You're real, aren't you? You're not a ghost?'

'I'm real.'

Faustina blinked and shook her head in bewilderment. 'So much to take in, so much to talk about... And who is this?' Her eyes travelled higher to take in the tall figure of Eprius, looming behind Isi.

'I am Eprius,' he said, with a polite bow of the head. 'An old friend of Lucius. I hope you don't mind me tagging along.'

'Of course not, come in, all of you.'

Faustina's modest apartment was pleasantly homely. The furnishings were simple but clean, and, in stark contrast to the stairwell, the rooms smelled of fresh flowers and citrus fruit.

She produced a plate of segmented oranges and invited her guests to sit on some wooden stools. The fruit looked juicy, and Lucius was hot and thirsty, but before he could tuck in, there was a question he simply had to ask.

'Valeria is safe and well,' Faustina said, anticipating his enquiry. 'She's living with your mother in Consul Glabrio's house on the Palatine.'

Lucius let out a long, slow breath of relief. 'Have you had any communication with her?'

Faustina shook her head. 'I only know what I know because I've talked to Glabrio's slaves at the market. Valeria hasn't been seen in public since the accident.'

'Accident?'

'Yes, the one on the Via Appia, when your carriage crashed into the marshes.'

Lucius nodded to himself. 'So that's how they're explaining it.'

'Explaining what? I'm sorry?'

'Yes, I fear I'm a little confused as well,' said Eprius. 'Who exactly are *they*, and what did they explain, to whom?'

Lucius exchanged a look with Isi. So far he'd only given Eprius a very brief and vague account of his recent adventures, with no mention of Praetorian guards or hooded assassins.

Isi shook her head vehemently at him, but Lucius ignored her. It was time, he decided, to come clean to both Faustina and Eprius.

When he'd finished telling his story, there was a lengthy silence. Eprius looked stunned – and Faustina looked furious. Unable to sit still, she bustled about, clearing plates and folding and refolding napkins. 'Glabrio is a monster,' she fumed. 'Worse than Ravilla. At least your uncle never sent assassins after you. I can't believe he ordered the murders of your brother and father...'

She began twisting a napkin in her hands, her knuckles white with tension. 'Now I understand why so few people came to your father's funeral. Your mother was there, of course, though without Valeria. And a few of your father's most loyal clients and freedmen and women showed up, including me. But I remember thinking at the time, *why wasn't it a grand occasion?* Why was there no laudatio delivered from the Rostra* in the Forum? Why no sacrifice as he was laid to rest in the family tomb? Your father was a great man – he did so much for this city, especially its poor. Where were the senators and patricians? Where indeed was Glabrio? Already, that monster must have started spreading his lies – making people think that your father was somehow dishonourable, a traitor to Rome – and all the cowards and fair-weather friends decided it was safer to stay away. I've heard the gossipmongers at the market say that Glabrio plans to marry your mother. I didn't think much about it till now, but of course it would mean that he'd legally take

---

* *laudatio: speech in praise of a dead person; Rostra: a platform, decorated with the prows (rostra) of captured enemy warships, from which public speeches were given.*

possession of all your father's lands and property. It's almost as if he wants to wipe your father out of existence.'

Lucius listened to this in impotent rage and grief, the taste of the orange turning to acid in his mouth. He felt tears prick his eyes, and angrily wiped them away.

'Glabrio couldn't downplay your brother's funeral, though,' continued Faustina, her voice lowered almost to a growl. 'He tried to – I see that now – by holding it at night. But he couldn't have anticipated the tens of thousands who turned out. The whole city came to pay their respects, or so it seemed. There were so many torches, Lucius, it was as though his body was carried along on a river of fire. It was beautiful. He was laid in an open casket, as many refused to believe the Phoenix of Pompeii could actually die. But it was Quin in there. I saw him with my own eyes. He looked like a young god…' She broke off, unable to continue.

Lucius took her hand and squeezed it softly. 'Thank you,' he said. 'I would have given anything to be at both funerals, but you've described them so well.'

Faustina threw down the napkin, bitterness contorting her features. 'Glabrio is a monster! He's destroyed two beautiful lives! He must be exposed! We must tell the world what he's done.'

'He may be a monster,' said Isi, 'but he's got the emperor and the Praetorian guard and the Senate and pretty much everyone else on his side. I don't think that telling the world he's a murderer will do much good. We might as well wear a big sign saying "Please execute us"!'

Faustina looked a little hurt by this scornful response from her friend, and she fell into a twitching, brooding sort of silence.

'We should be bold,' said Eprius. 'We should go and visit Glabrio at his house. It's the last thing he'll expect. He'll get the shock of his life seeing Lucius alive, but he would never attack him in front of his mother and sister.'

'Who's to say what Glabrio would or wouldn't do?' said Isi. 'The man's completely ruthless.'

Ignoring her, Eprius turned to Lucius, his eyes growing brighter as the idea solidified in his mind. 'He'll feel obliged to welcome you with open arms. You'll be invited to stay, of course. You'll pretend ignorance of his crimes – so he won't be wary of you. And once you're inside his house, you're sure to find an opportunity to kill him.'

'That's a terrible idea,' said Isi. 'Lucius's one advantage is that everyone, including Glabrio, thinks he's dead, and you want to throw that away by encouraging him to walk straight into the lion's den and announce himself. Glabrio will order his guards to kill him before he can get two steps inside the door – long before his mother and sister ever get to see him. The one thing that can possibly threaten Glabrio is Lucius being alive – of course he'll kill him, without a second's hesitation.'

'Well, what do you think we should do, then?' snapped Lucius, who had actually liked Eprius's idea.

Isi looked at her hands and began chipping away at a broken nail. 'We shouldn't rush into anything. We should lie low for a while and keep a check on Glabrio's movements. Faustina goes to the market every day. She's got an ear for the gossip. Three of us are trained killers. If we're patient, we'll find an opportunity to catch him unawares. All it takes is a moment.'

'We could wait forever for such a moment,' said Eprius. 'I remember in Pompeii, the duovirs* wouldn't go anywhere without an armed escort. Roman consuls must be even better protected.'

'That's exactly what you said when we discussed this on the ship, remember?' Lucius said to Isi. 'You know an attack on him in public is impossible, admit it!'

'Not as impossible as what Eprius is suggesting,' retorted Isi.

'I'm not so sure,' said Lucius. 'I think the bold approach might just work. As Eprius says, it's the last thing Glabrio would expect. I could play the innocent – claim I've come to be reunited with my remaining family. He may not be aware that I met Canio and that I know the truth about him – it depends on whether that hooded fellow has got a message to him yet. Either way, he'll have no choice but to welcome me. Then, once I get Val on her own, she'll be able to give me all the vital inside information I need – she'll know when

* *duovirs: the two chief magistrates (law officers) of the city.*

he's most vulnerable. Together we'll figure out a way of killing him.'

'It's a suicide mission,' said Isi with a dismissive shake of her head. 'It's like heading into Medusa's lair without a mirror.'*

Lucius was starting to get seriously impatient with Isi. What had got into her lately? Why did she constantly feel the need to put him and his ideas down? Ever since that stop-off in Crete, she'd grown increasingly headstrong and domineering – always believing she knew better. Did she think he was a little child in need of her protection? More than a few times, he'd bitten his tongue to avoid an argument. But this time she'd gone too far.

'Who do you think you are – my mother?' he shouted at her. Isi stared back, and he was pleased to see the hurt surprise forming on her face. He stood over her and suddenly twelve days of pent-up resentment started pouring out of him. 'I know what this is,' he ranted. 'This is jealousy! You're jealous of my friendship with Eprius. Ever since he turned up, you've been trying to come between us, or turn me against him. You can't stand the fact that he's had a good idea – an idea that actually has a chance of success!'

Lucius sat down to a stunned silence. Faustina was the first to speak. 'Can I get anyone anything else?' she

---

* *Medusa's lair: in Greek and Roman myth, Medusa was a gorgon – a monstrous woman with snakes for hair. Anyone who looked her in the face was turned to stone, but the hero Perseus avoided this fate by looking at her reflection in a polished shield.*

offered in a quavering voice. 'Bread? Cheese? Olives?'

Lucius didn't reply and nor did Isi. They just stared at each other like two angry bulls.

Finally, Eprius rose to his feet. 'Perhaps it's time I got going,' he said with a nervous grin. 'I mean, it's been wonderful and all, seeing you again, Lucius, and to meet you, Isi, and you, Faustina. But, well, I've got things to do – find some accommodation, register myself at a ludus, that sort of thing. So perhaps it's better if I just, er… push off.'

'No,' said Lucius, keeping his eyes fixed on Isi. 'Stay, Eprius. He's welcome to stay, isn't he, Faustina?'

'Of course,' she said in a tight voice. 'For as long as he wants. Now, are you sure I can't get anyone some…'

Isi stood up abruptly, knocking over the stool she'd been sitting on. She almost ran into a smaller room, then slumped on the narrow bed, her hands covering her face. Faustina immediately went to join her there, placing a comforting arm around her shoulder.

It annoyed Lucius that Isi preferred to sulk rather than own up to her jealousy. He maintained a good-humoured smile for Eprius's sake. 'It'll be all right,' he murmured to him. 'She'll come round to it.'

Eprius fiddled with his orange peel and said nothing.

'Are you happy staying here?' Lucius asked. 'I mean, until you get yourself sorted out at a ludus?'

'Maybe it's not such a good idea,' said Eprius with a frown. 'You have an important and difficult task on your hands, and I'd just get in the way.'

'Are you sure?' said Lucius, suddenly trying to come up with reasons why Eprius should stay. 'Will you be OK on your own? You don't know anyone, and you don't know your way around yet.' He began to wonder whether his desire to help Eprius was motivated by guilt, or whether he simply enjoyed his company.

'I'll be fine, Lucius,' Eprius assured him, 'although I'd appreciate it if you'd show me the way to the Ludus Romanus. You mentioned the lanista there – Crassus? I'd like to introduce myself to him.'

Lucius accepted defeat with a nod of the head. 'I'd be happy to,' he said. 'We can go there now if you like.'

He went into the bedroom. Isi looked up, her face tense and pale. She seemed to be waiting for an apology, but Lucius didn't feel he owed her one – he certainly didn't want her to think she'd won the argument or anything. 'You'll be glad to hear Eprius is going,' he told her. 'I'm going to take him over to the Ludus Romanus now.'

'Take him there and then come straight back,' she warned him. 'Keep your head down and don't talk to anyone.'

'Of course, that's exactly what I planned to do,' said Lucius stiffly. He hated that older-sisterish tone.

'See you later, Lucius,' said Faustina. 'Good luck, Eprius! Nice to have met you!'

Lucius and Eprius walked south along the Vicus Longus,[*] and soon entered the neighbourhood of Suburra. For eleven months Lucius had been a resident of these narrow, filthy streets, but he hadn't been back since and had almost forgotten how threatening they felt, even in daylight. Shadowy figures bustled by, reeking of cheap wine, and Lucius tensed in readiness for an attack whenever a stranger met his eyes. Grubby, barefooted children clustered around their feet, offering themselves as guides, messengers, porters or litter bearers. Shrivelled beggars, many of them blind or lame, sat in doorways holding out their hands for a coin.

Eprius barely noticed the squalor, keeping his eyes fixed on the skyline. He sighed with awe as the Flavian Amphitheatre came into view above the ugly tenement rooftops, looking like a curving multi-tiered cliff of stone. Its travertine limestone exterior was the colour of honey in the April sunshine, and from the topmost tier, colourful banners fluttered against the blue sky.

Lucius envied Eprius his innocence. For Lucius, the sight of the amphitheatre always brought to mind images of screaming, blood-soaked animals. To Eprius, he imagined, it must appear like a palace of dreams.

'You could be fighting there very soon,' he smiled, hoping Eprius wouldn't hear the sadness in his voice. Then he stopped, conscious of the danger of being recognised. 'You should be able to find your own

---

[*] *Vicus Longus: 'long street', located between the Viminal and Quirinal hills.*

way from here,' he said. 'The Ludus Romanus is just beyond the amphitheatre. When you speak to Crassus, tell him you knew me in Pompeii, but for Jove's sake* don't let on that I'm still alive.'

Eprius laughed. 'Thank you, Lucius – for everything.' They clasped wrists and embraced.

'Salvete,** friends!' came a gruff voice behind them. 'Travellers, are you? Your first time in Rome?'

'We don't want a guide, thanks,' said Lucius, turning on the stranger.

He was a grizzled-looking man with a stoop. His face, framed by a straggly grey beard, had the leathery look of a life spent on the streets, and he was dressed in a filthy old trabea – a red toga more commonly worn by priests and augurs.***

'Then let me be a guide to your future,' said the man, producing a crooked wand from beneath the folds of his trabea and giving a small bow. 'Gentlemen, I offer you the benefit of my years of study at the College of Augurs on the Palatine. I am officially qualified to read auspices from the weather, birds, dogs, foxes, horses, and most other quadrupeds; unusual events, rumblings in the earth, strange lights in the sky, swarms of bees – you name your sign, and I'll interpret the will of the

---

* for Jove's sake: Jove is another name for Jupiter, father of the gods.

** Salvete: greetings.

*** augurs: priests who claimed to be able to interpret the will of the gods by observing natural phenomena such as the flight of birds. The signs they observed were known as auspices.

gods from it.' He spoke so fast, Lucius and Eprius had no chance to interrupt. 'Seen anything odd lately?' the man went on. 'A freakish-looking animal, perchance? Just step this way, and I'll explain all.' He began ushering Lucius and Eprius towards a dingy-looking hovel, propped against the wall of a tenement building a few paces down a side alley.

Lucius tried to shrug him off. 'Take your hands off me, you old charlatan!' he said. 'You're no augur, or you wouldn't be living like a beggar.'

'Don't be deceived by appearances,' chuckled the man. 'If I have spurned a life of luxury, it is only the better to pursue my art…'

'And to pursue helpless bystanders on street corners!' cried Lucius. The beggar was proving surprisingly strong and difficult to shake off.

'Just get away from us, you awful man!' shouted Eprius, drawing a dagger from his belt.

Instead of retreating as they had expected, the man ignored the blade and flourished his wand, drawing an invisible rectangle in the air above their heads. He squinted into the distance, then flinched in alarm. 'Ravens circling atop the amphitheatre! Alas! Bad things are coming your way, unless you come with me now.'

The wand twitched, and Eprius yelped as his hand received a thwack and the dagger spun through the air to land in the beggar's other fist. The movement had been too quick for either of them to see. In a rage, Eprius rushed at the old man – then stopped and keeled over backwards, clutching his jaw, his mouth a circle of shock and pain. Again, if the man had struck him, it had been too swift for Lucius to make out.

A hard gleam replaced the charming twinkle in the beggar's eyes, as he jabbed the knife in the direction of his lean-to. 'Step inside, gentlemen,' he said in a voice that had lost all of its honey charm. Briefly, Lucius considered using his own dagger to fight him off. But the beggar seemed to read his thoughts. He glanced at the dagger hilt, then caught Lucius's eye and shook his head.

The flimsy shack looked to have been constructed from assorted materials that had fallen off wagons and rooftops: nailed-together timber planking, canvas sheeting and broken clay tiles. In one corner lay a filthy sleeping mat, a threadbare coverlet and a cracked oil lamp. On a little table in another corner were the remains of the man's breakfast: a cup of watered vinegar and a lump of hard cheese.

'What do you want with us?' demanded Eprius as soon as they were inside. He was forced to crouch beneath the low roof, and nearly tripped on a wooden chest lying next to the sleeping mat.

The man stood in front of the door, barring their way in case either was thinking about escape.

'I know what he wants,' said Lucius, wearily opening his leather pouch and offering their captor the few coins he had. 'This is all rather elaborate for a mugging, isn't it, old man?' he remarked. 'You could have just demanded our money and been done with it.'

The man ignored Lucius's coins. 'Pass me the bowl of water on top of that chest, will you?' he said to Eprius.

When Eprius had handed it to him, the man fished a sponge out of the bowl and began dabbing at his face.

'I don't want your money, Lucius,' he said.

Lucius shook when he heard his name, and the horrid thought struck him that this was all a trap: the fake augur was an agent of Glabrio's – maybe the same hooded assassin who had killed his father and then nearly killed him in Ephesus.

'How do you know my name?' he demanded through gritted teeth, trying to keep the tremor out of his voice.

It was more than just street grime, he noticed, coming off on the sponge – it looked like some sort of greasy brown paint as well – and it revealed fresh, youthful skin beneath.

'Why shouldn't I know your name?' With a grimace, the fellow pulled off his beard, which turned out to have been glued to his chin. And beneath the grey wig were curly gold locks, dark with sweat.

'After all,' he laughed, 'I am your brother.'

CHAPTER XII

18 APRIL

s Lucius stared at the man facing him, the whole world seemed to wobble and tilt. His vision grew blurry and the floor slid away from beneath his feet. He was tipping, toppling, falling. He put out his hands, but everything was melting – nothing was solid. 'No! No!' he heard himself cry. 'You're dead! I saw you die!'

Hands grasped him as he fell. Lucius stared again at the man who now looked like Quin. 'I saw you rushing into those soldiers!' he yelled at him. 'They cut you down!'

The man held him, frowning with concern. 'Lucius! Are you OK?' There were strands of false beard still stuck to his chin.

'Thousands saw your body at the funeral!' Lucius told him. 'You cannot be alive.'

'I can explain everything,' the Quin lookalike said to him. 'Just give me a chance!'

Lucius tried to wriggle out of his grip. 'No, you're a ghost, or... or someone who looks like my brother... This can't be happening.' He rubbed his eyes and blinked, trying to make the nonsensical vision go away – but Quin remained there, smiling down at him.

'Here, drink this!' he said, handing him a chipped mug of water.

Lucius drank a deep draught and his head began to clear. He looked again at the familiar face, and the fear slowly began to fade. A warm glow suffused his stomach. However crazy and ridiculous, this vision of his brother, full of all his old life and humour, was persisting – it wasn't a dream. The warmth gradually grew in intensity until it became a hot flood of joy that flushed his cheeks deep red and sent a prickling sensation through every hair on his head.

It really was Quin!

He set down the cup, threw his arms around his brother's neck and wept.

'How?' he gasped, when he could speak again. 'How are you still alive?'

'I could ask the same about you,' said Quin, his voice also husky with emotion. 'You have an engraved stone in the family tomb, just as I do.'

'Yes, but there's no body beneath mine,' said Lucius.

'True,' conceded Quin. 'Of the two of us, I am possibly more dead than you.'

Lucius laughed, and wiped the tears from his eyes.

'Sir,' said Eprius, stepping forward. 'I am pleased and honoured to make your acquaintance. I'm Eprius, a friend of Lucius – originally from Pompeii, where I had the privilege of seeing you fight. I see now why they call you the Phoenix.'*

Quin smiled at Eprius's awkward formality. 'Salve, Eprius,' he said affably.

'You have to tell us how you survived,' Lucius demanded. 'Is there a rational explanation, or were the myth-makers right after all when they said you cannot die?'

'I'm not sure,' chuckled Quin, removing the last remnants of his disguise with the help of an old bronze mirror. 'Perhaps the legend helped a little... When I charged at those Praetorians on the causeway seven months ago, I fully expected to die. My only aim was to create a brief diversion, so that you and Val could get away. As I fell into the front ranks, the soldiers were so shocked they didn't get a clean swipe at me, but one of them caught me on the forehead with the flat of his sword. I collapsed unconscious, and they were about to run me through, but the centurion in charge stopped them. He recognised me, you see, from

---

* *Phoenix: in Greek myth, a bird that was repeatedly destroyed by fire and then born again from the ashes. Quin was given this nickname because of his many escapes from death in the arena.*

my days as a gladiator. It turned out he was a huge fan. When I regained consciousness, the centurion told me he would allow me to choose the method of my execution – as a mark of respect. He wished he didn't have to kill me at all, but he said he had no choice, what with his superior demanding to see my dead body. So I said to him, why don't you show your superior a different body? I already had one in mind. You remember Ennius, the servant sent to fetch us? – the one who looked a little like me?'

Lucius nodded, suddenly understanding: 'So it was Ennius he showed to his superior! And it was Ennius in the open casket at your funeral…'

'You have it! They retrieved the young man's corpse from that little shop where we were held captive, and I gave them the address of an old friend of mine called Mutio – a master of make-up and disguise. The games organisers often make use of his services in battle re-enactments, to make Romans look like Gallic or Germanic tribesmen – that's how I met him. Mutio made up the corpse to look almost identical to me. By the time he'd finished, I'd challenge anyone to spot the difference, even Mother. The centurion was satisfied, and he set me free on condition that I never again set foot in Rome. Of course, that was a promise I could not keep… Not after the centurion had told me the name of the man who had ordered our deaths…'

'Consul Glabrio,' said Lucius.

'You know, then! Were you as shocked as I was?

The man who posed as our saviour all those months ago! Little did we know he was luring us into a trap! How did you find out it was him?'

'I'll tell you later. First finish your story.'

'Once I knew who our enemy was, I began to make plans to kill him, and rescue Mother and Valeria. Mutio taught me all about his craft. Then I set myself up here on the streets of Suburra, in the guise of a down-at-heel augur, watching and waiting for my chance...'

'Do you ever see Glabrio out on the streets?' asked Eprius.

'Yes, he makes his regular visits to the Senate house, always taking the same route, and always surrounded by his twelve beefy lictors. He's a creature of habit, is Glabrio.'

'What about gaining access to his house?' inquired Lucius.

'It's impregnable – high walls, iron bars over the windows, constantly patrolled by guards.'

'Do you have any news of Mother and Val?'

Quin shook his head. 'I don't know whether they're prisoners or house guests, or whether they know the truth about Glabrio. They never go out. In fact, the only time I've seen Mother was at my own funeral.'

'You were there?'

Quin smirked. 'How could I miss it? The whole city was there.' He eyed his brother with affection. 'It's so great to see you again, Lu. I almost didn't recognise you just now as you walked by. With all those muscles, you could qualify as a lictor yourself – or a gladiator, even...'

'Well, it's funny you should say that...' smiled Lucius, and he began to relate his own story.

Quin laughed with astonishment when he heard how Lucius had evaded death in the marshes, and beamed in admiration at his subsequent adventures as a gladiator in Carthage and Ephesus. The story of Canio and the hooded assassin left him disturbed. 'Do you think this assassin might have followed you back here?' he asked.

Lucius shrugged. 'I don't even know if we're talking about one person. There might be a team of killers working for Glabrio. We need to be on our guard in any case. By now, the man in Ephesus may have got a message to Glabrio that I'm still alive and possibly in Rome.'

'I still think your best plan would be to approach Glabrio openly,' said Eprius. 'Maybe I'm being innocent, but why don't both of you just march up to his house and demand entry...? Back in Pompeii, I thought I was powerless against Valens. For months I submitted to his blackmail and the beatings of his street thugs because I believed I had no choice. Now I realise I could have destroyed the man's power over me in an instant simply by confessing all to my father. These men thrive on secrets. Openness is the key.'

Quin shook his head. 'I'd normally be the first to argue for that approach, but not in this case. We're not dealing with a Ravilla or a Valens here. This man thinks nothing of killing his enemies in cold blood. And the stakes are so much higher for Glabrio. He's a Consul of Rome in danger of being exposed as the murderer of Titus, who is now a god! He will go to any lengths to prevent that, even if it means cutting us down in his own vestibule in full sight of our mother and sister... No, I have a plan – a much better plan...'

Quin lowered his voice as he said this last bit, and Lucius and Eprius instinctively moved closer.

'Glabrio is sponsoring six days of games at the Flavian Amphitheatre, starting tomorrow, to celebrate the 835th birthday of the city of Rome. There will be gladiator fights in the afternoons, and one of those gladiators – in disguise, of course – will be me...'

'But you swore you'd never fight again!' interjected Lucius. 'And how can this possibly help us in our plan?'

'Patience, brother,' laughed Quin. 'Let me explain everything, and then I'll hear your objections... I told you earlier that Glabrio is a creature of habit, and it so happens that it's his habit to meet with victors of gladiator bouts afterwards, in his box, so that he can personally congratulate them. I'm confident that I'll be one of those winners. He'll have his lictors around him, of course, and I won't be able to bring my sword in with me, but for a few brief seconds I'll be within touching distance of him... If I could sneak in a very small dagger – embedded, say, in the sole of my sandal – and if I'm very quick, I'll get a chance to strike.

I'll be killed immediately, of course, but at least I'll die knowing I've avenged Father.'

All the air went out of Lucius when he heard this, and fresh tears pricked his eyes – but not the joyful ones of earlier. The euphoria he'd felt fell away like a retreating tide. He should have been happy that Father was going to be avenged. Killing Glabrio was all he wanted from life. So why did he now feel so empty inside?

'I don't want to lose you, Quin,' he groaned. 'Not even for this. I've only just got you back!'

Quin gripped his shoulder. 'I'm doing it for Father,' he said, sadness shadowing his smile. 'And for all of us. This is for our family's honour. And what is life worth without that, hm? Be strong. Be proud. Tomorrow, we'll win back our name!'

Lucius shook his head, his face tight. An idea had been forming in his head even while Quin was speaking. He was forgetting his own destiny: he was a weapon! This was for him to do – not Quin.

'It won't work if you do it,' he said slowly.

'What do you mean?'

'You're too well known in this city... You'll be fighting in front of thousands of your old fans. However well you disguise yourself, you're bound to be recognised – they'll know you from your style! If Glabrio gets wind that it's you, he won't let you near him – he'll have you quietly killed in the tunnel as you're escorted from the arena. I, on the other hand, am completely unknown in this city. I should do this, not you…'

'I can disguise my style,' said Quin, his eyes feverishly bright. 'I'll fight left-handed if I have to, by Jove!'

Lucius shook his head. 'You'll struggle to win if you don't fight in your natural way... You may struggle anyway. Think about it – you haven't picked up your net and trident in over two years. You're rusty, Quin. While you've been wandering the streets waving your lituus* at passers-by, I've been in intensive training… I'm quick, and lethal. If you want this to happen – if you really want Father to be avenged – you have to let me do this!'

'No!' cried Quin, tears forming in his eyes. Lucius knew he'd won the argument – it was only Quin's pride, and his brotherly love, that prevented him from accepting the facts. 'I'm the eldest son,' said Quin. It's my duty to avenge Father.'

'It's your duty to be head of the family,' countered Lucius. 'That's what Father would have wanted. You have to survive in order to protect and provide for Mother and Valeria.'

Quin gazed at him with a strange mixture of sadness and awe. 'You've really grown up, haven't you, little brother?'

---

* *lituus: augur's wand.*

The wooden chest on the floor of Quin's shack contained a rack of cosmetic bottles he'd purchased from his friend Mutio. They included plant juices, seeds, pieces of horn, animal excrement and urine, honey, vinegar, bile, sulphur, myrrh, ground oyster shells, poultry fat, white lead, chalk powder, beeswax, olive oil, rosewater and starch. These were used for darkening, whitening or ageing skin, concealing or adding facial marks, and softening or accentuating features. There were also resin pastes and pumice stones for stripping off hair and smoothing skin, and an assortment of wigs, beards, false ears, false noses, and costumes. Lucius was impressed. With this box of tricks, his brother could become virtually anybody he wanted.

Quin picked out a bottle of swan fat, which he applied to Lucius's cheeks to reduce the rosiness of his brother's complexion. He used ashes of snail shells to harden the line of his cheek bones, and applied kohl to his eyelashes to darken them. He used antimony to extend his eyebrows inwards so they almost met in the centre, and pasted a soft leather patch to his forehead to give the appearance of an old childhood scar. The disguise was capped off with a wig of thick black hair to conceal Lucius's unruly brown mop.

Quin stood back to admire his handiwork. 'All you need now is a name,' he said.

'I have one,' responded Lucius immediately. 'I'm Alecto.'

'OK, Alecto,' sighed Quin. 'You're safe to go and register now, and I defy anyone from the Ludus Romanus or the Morning School, or any of your old stomping grounds, to recognise you.

'A remarkable transformation!' gasped Eprius.

Lucius checked himself out in Quin's mirror, and had to agree. 'I look older and tougher,' he said, twisting his mouth into a mean-looking sneer.

'I don't know what effect you'll have on your opponents, but you frighten the life out of me,' smiled Quin. 'Come back here tomorrow, before the fight, and I'll freshen up your disguise.'

Appius Seius Crassus, lanista of the Ludus Romanus, stood on the sand of the practice arena and eyed the two young gladiators standing before him. He wore the appraising look of a dairy farmer sizing up a pair of heifers. Lucius stared straight ahead, careful not to meet his former boss's eye. Beads of sweat broke out on his forehead as he sensed Crassus peering closely at his face. Did he recognise him under the make-up and the wig? He prayed the kohl around his eyes wouldn't run – if he was identified now, their whole scheme would fall apart. After a prolonged stare, the lanista's gaze fell away.

Crassus was short and stocky – a fearsome Provocator in his day – with narrow, cold eyes and a face that looked carved from granite. Eprius towered over him, yet there was no question that Crassus was the more imposing figure. His employers may have changed with the seasons – Ravilla, Aquila and now Glabrio – but Crassus was a permanent fixture, and his solid, scowling presence somehow symbolised the Ludus Romanus in the way its owners never would.

'Well, you both look all right to me,' he said gruffly. 'Now let's see how you fight.' He handed them each a wooden sword, weighted with iron. 'Whenever you're ready!' he growled.

It was Lucius's first experience of sparring with Eprius. The young man had a quick, fluid style, based on fast footwork, agile movements and a strong, flexible wrist. He also benefited from a long reach, and Lucius had to skip smartly out of range when he attacked. He could see how Eprius had made primus palus at Gortyn – he would have been a formidable opponent for anyone at the Carthage school as well. Nevertheless, Lucius couldn't help noticing one small giveaway: Eprius always took a tiny sip of breath just before he lunged – a warning signal for Lucius to parry. Was he doing this deliberately to help his friend, or was it a weakness?

Overall, they seemed well-matched, with neither able to find a way through the other's defences. Of course, Lucius knew very well that a sparring session could only tell you so much about a fighter. Lucius was holding quite a bit back in terms of aggression, and he sensed that Eprius was, too. He truly hoped he wouldn't have to find out how he measured up against him in a real contest. If his plan was to work, Lucius needed an opponent he could be sure of beating, and he wasn't sure he could beat Eprius. He held him in such affection that he might struggle to summon up the necessary hatred to defeat him. And if he did manage this, and Eprius died, that would be awful – he wanted his friend to lead a long, happy life.

After five minutes, Crassus clapped his hands, signalling them to stop. 'OK, you've impressed me. Welcome, both of you, to our familia. Your arrival here is well-timed, with the anniversary games starting tomorrow. I'm putting you both down to fight on the opening afternoon.' None of this was said with much warmth, but it cheered Lucius nonetheless – the first stage of the plan was in place.

Crassus led his new recruits back to his office, then went through the terms with them: he offered them a five-year contract worth 4,000 sestertii, with 2,000 sestertii paid up front – the usual sum offered to Auctorati.

Eprius started to ask how many times he could expect to fight in a year, but Crassus raised his hand, stopping him in mid-flow. 'Once you're sworn in, my boy, you're my property to be disposed of as I see fit. I don't negotiate appearance frequency or anything else with gladiators. If you're still alive five years from now, I'll release you from your contract and you'll be a free man again. Until that time, you belong to me, body and soul. Understood?'

Eprius nodded meekly and signed the contract. Lucius knew that this time tomorrow he'd be dead, so what did he care about contracts? Before he signed, however, he asked if he could spend his last night of freedom with his family. He had to say goodbye to Quin and Isi before he fought.

Crassus grumbled a little at this request, but eventually acceded. 'Mark you, if you're not here by the second hour of the day, according to the sundial in the main quadrangle, you'll be on punishment rations for a week. And that wouldn't be a good start to your career here, now would it?'

He summoned an attendant as witness, then Lucius and Eprius held up their right hands and recited the sacramentum gladiatorum – the gladiators' oath – officially consigning themselves to a state of servitude. 'I swear to give over my body to be burned, flogged, beaten or slain by cold steel, according to my owner's wishes...' Lucius spoke the words impassively, barely registering their meaning.

Crassus told the attendant to show Eprius to his dormitory. Eprius mouthed a farewell to Lucius before departing. Lucius was about to head out himself when the lanista called him back.

'Alecto, a word, please – in private.'

With a shudder, Lucius re-entered the office, closing the door behind him.

Crassus examined him curiously for a few moments, and once again Lucius feared the worst. He watched, mesmerised, as the lanista's broad index finger traced slow patterns in the gnarled surface of his limewood desk, and he waited for the words, full of bonhomie and menace: *Hello, Lucius*.

'An old friend of mine,' said Crassus eventually, 'an alumnus* of this school, name of Gracchus – he runs the ludus in Carthage these days. Have you heard of him?'

Lucius's heart sank. Whether he was identified as himself or as an escaped slave, it made little difference: his plan was foiled, either way.

'No, sir,' he said as innocently as he could.

'He's put word out that a slave gladiator, a Hoplomachus by the name of Alecto, has escaped from his school. That wouldn't be you by any chance?'

'No, sir.' He could feel a rivulet of sweat sliding down his cheek like a gleaming badge of guilt.

Crassus laughed – a harsh bark that Lucius remembered only too well. 'I suppose an escaped slave gladiator is hardly going to sign himself back into servitude as an Auctoratus, now, is he? That would be absurd…'

'Yes, sir.' Lucius was careful to keep his face impassive, despite Crassus's smile. This could still be a trap.

The lanista's face relapsed into its more habitual

* *alumnus: former pupil.*

frown. 'Unless there was some particular reason why he wanted to come here...'

Lucius waited, hardly able to breathe.

Crassus stared at him for what seemed like forever. Finally, the lanista nodded to himself, muttering something about coincidences, and telling Lucius he was free to leave.

Lucius silently blessed Fortuna, the goddess of good and bad luck, as he made his way back through the streets towards the Quirinal Hill. Crassus's need for new fighters evidently overrode his suspicions about 'Alecto'. Still, his old boss definitely looked doubtful and Lucius would have to be on his guard tomorrow.

When he got back to Faustina's insula, Isi was waiting there in the ground-floor entrance, hands on hips. Her face was pink with fury and she looked like a very short Vesuvius. 'What took you so long?' she fumed. 'You were only supposed to take him there and come straight back.' Then she could no longer control herself and she hugged him with all her considerable strength. 'I thought you were dead,' she murmured.

'I have news,' said Lucius, slightly breathless from the hug. 'Amazing news. Quin's alive!'

She staggered back from him. 'No! Impossible!'

'I wouldn't have believed it myself if I hadn't seen him with my own eyes!'

She stared at Lucius a moment, her eyes aglow with surprise and delight, and it seemed to him that she was the old Isi again, and that they could go back to being friends. Knowing he was to die tomorrow, he wanted this more than anything. Isi pulled him off the street into the more private space of the vestibule. 'Tell me everything,' she said.

Lucius obliged, recounting the details of the meeting with Quin, but leaving out the plan for a suicide attack – he didn't want to bring down the mood just yet. He expected her to be happy to hear about Quin, so was puzzled by her frown when he finished.

'Eprius witnessed everything, then?' she said.

'Of course. He was so proud to meet Quin. You should have heard him...' Lucius stopped when he saw her expression. 'What's wrong, Isi?'

'That boy worries me, he really does.'

Lucius sighed. He'd hoped that she'd finally decided to let go of her ridiculous suspicions about Eprius. 'What is it about him you don't like? He's never been anything but perfectly charming to you, and yet you act as though he's some kind of street robber who'd slit our throats at the first opportunity.'

She pressed her lips together and contemplated the ceiling as if trying to decide whether to reveal something. Eventually, she said in a low voice: 'I knew there was something not right about him from the very first. You remember that day in Chersonasos when we came back to the ship and found him on deck?'

'Of course.'

'I spoke to him in Greek.'

'Yes, you seemed to be getting on very well, I thought.'

'We were – though I noticed something at the time, and it bothered me...'

'What was that?'

'Well, he was fluent enough, but he spoke the kind of Greek that's taught to Roman schoolboys by classically trained tutors – Athenian Greek, basically, as might have been spoken hundreds of years ago by Plato or Aristotle* – not the rough, slangy Greek that he'd have picked up if he'd spent spent two years in the Gortyn ludus, as he claimed.'

'Are you saying he lied to us?'

Isi frowned. 'I wasn't sure at first. But now, after the way he was talking today, I am.'

'What do you mean?'

'I mean the way he was encouraging you to go and see Glabrio.'

'I happen to think that was quite a good plan,' said Lucius.

'A good plan if you're Eprius, maybe.'

Lucius stared at her, now totally perplexed. 'What are you talking about?'

'Listen,' said Isi. 'Eprius wasn't a gladiator in Gortyn. In fact, I don't think he'd spent any time on Crete. I reckon he was on that ship all along. He must

* *Plato, Aristotle: famous Greek philosophers of the 5th and 4th centuries BC.*

have come on board at Ephesus – probably while we were in the harbour buying provisions for the journey – and spent the whole of the first part of the voyage in his cabin below decks, so we never saw him.'

'But why?' exploded Lucius. 'Why would he hide from us, and then lie about coming aboard at Crete?'

Isi looked nervous, as if anxious about the effect her next words might have. 'Because, Lucius, I'm convinced that your friend Eprius is one of Glabrio's spies.'

Lucius turned away from her with a bitter laugh. 'You can't mean that, Isi!'

'He has the same build as the hooded figure I saw in the street outside Canio's place,' she said urgently. 'And the one I saw hanging around the lion's cage in the arena – they were both tall, like him, with the same loose-limbed way of moving.'

'Isi, this is crazy... Eprius is my friend. He can't possibly –'

'And that's not all,' she interrupted. 'Remember that time he challenged you to dive into the water and scrape barnacles off the steering oar?'

'What about it?' said Lucius wearily.

'The sailor clearly told him there were sharks in the water, but Eprius ignored that bit. And when I mentioned it, he claimed he didn't even know what a shark was. But how could a boy who grew up in a coastal town like Pompeii, and then spent two years on an island, not know what a shark was?'

Lucius laughed. 'So now you're saying Eprius was trying to get me eaten by a shark?'

'Of course he was – only you're too stubborn to see it! He was always trying to find some way of getting you on your own during the voyage, so he could bundle you overboard – the only way I could stop him was by sticking to you like Echo to Narcissus,* remember?'

'I remember,' said Lucius grimly.

'When Eprius dared you to dive in that day, it was another assassination attempt! If he couldn't get a lion to eat you, then maybe a shark would oblige!'

For all her crazy paranoia, Lucius couldn't help feeling moved by what Isi was saying. She obviously cared a lot about him, and her clinginess on the trip hadn't been prompted by jealousy, but by fear that he might get killed.

He smiled gently. 'Isi, you didn't have to worry. Eprius isn't what you think he is. He's a good friend. I saved his life in Pompeii, getting him out of the city just before it was destroyed. He owes me! The last thing he'd ever want to do is hurt me. But thank you… Thank you for trying to save me. I appreciate it!'

Isi looked down, blushing. 'You think I'm a fool, right?'

'No, I think you're a fantastic friend who cares about me, and I don't deserve you.' He laughed. 'Though I

* *like Echo to Narcissus: in Greek mythology, the mountain spirit Echo fell in love with the handsome mortal Narcissus, but he rejected her.*

notice you let me go off with the assassin all alone just now… I suppose I deserved that after what I said to you before.'

'Who says I did?' she smiled. 'I shadowed you all the way to Suburra, you fool.'

'You didn't!'

She nodded, blushing again. 'But then I lost you. I suppose that must have been when Quin dragged you into his shack. I've been worried sick ever since.'

'Well, you didn't need to be.'

'And the Greek thing. How do you explain that?'

'He's from a wealthy patrician background,' said Lucius. 'He probably did learn classical Greek as a child, and that's what he used while he was in Gortyn. You've heard how he speaks Latin – streetwise language just doesn't rub off on him. I'm sure the Cretan gladiators found him very amusing. And his aristo background also explains his ignorance of sharks. He may have grown up in Pompeii, but I'm sure he never spoke to a single fisherman. Those patricians live in their own isolated little world of privilege. I remember – I lived like that myself once.'

'I've been an idiot,' said Isi miserably. 'I'm sorry.' She looked at him. 'Will you ever forgive me?'

'I already have,' beamed Lucius. 'And I'm sorry for saying you were jealous earlier.'

'Perhaps I was – a bit,' she admitted.

Lucius smiled. 'So was I when I watched you joking around with Felix.'

'You weren't!' she laughed.

'I'm afraid I was.'

'You fool,' she said, giving him a hug. 'You'll always be my best friend.'

Lucius felt a tug of sorrow then as he remembered that this was really their last goodbye. His body trembled as he whispered her name. 'Isi, I've got something to tell you. It'll make you sad at first, but I hope you'll also understand, in time, that it's a good thing, and you'll be happy for me...'

Her head jerked up. He watched the tears forming in her eyes – she knew what he was about to say.

CHAPTER XIII

19 APRIL

ucius woke up before dawn on the floor of Faustina's living room. He didn't wake Faustina, or Isi, who was sharing her bedroom. Isi had asked him to, but he reckoned that they'd said all that needed saying the night before, and he didn't relish a drawn-out and painful goodbye. Shivering with tension as much as cold, he got dressed in the frail light of a single oil lamp.

The first salmon-coloured rays of dawn were appearing above the insulae on the Viminal Hill as he made his way along the Vicus Longus. Shopkeepers were pulling up their shutters and the usual din of the day – the tapping of coppersmiths, the sawing and hammering of carpenters and the chiselling of stonecutters – had already begun. Lucius stopped at a bakery to buy a loaf that he and Quin could share for their breakfast – not that he felt the slightest bit hungry. His stomach was a tight ball of tension as he contemplated the multitude of practical difficulties that lay between him and his goal: What if he lost to his opponent? What if someone saw him taking the knife out of his sandal? What if he couldn't get near enough to Glabrio? What if he only wounded him?

The inevitable consequence of his attack – his own messy, painful death – didn't frighten him half so much as the possibility of failing to kill the consul. Any desire he'd once had for a normal, happy existence had vanished the day his father was killed. In the swamp he'd vowed to dedicate what remained of his life to revenge. Ever since then he'd been preparing himself for this day, and now it was here, he didn't fear death, only failure to fulfil his duty.

That's what he told himself, anyway. But if he was honest, he didn't know how he'd feel, really, with a dozen sword-brandishing lictors bearing down on him. He'd probably be terrified, but at the same time ecstatic (if it was possible to feel both those things simultaneously) because hopefully by that time Glabrio would be bleeding to death at his feet.

He wished Isi could have been more positive when they'd discussed it all last night. He'd explained to her that this was always going to be his destiny, and that she should be happy for him. But all she could do was cry and, between sobs, ask him how he could possibly expect her to be happy that her best friend was about to die. Faustina had cried, too. All in all, it had been a depressing evening. In time, he kept telling himself – in time they'd understand that this was the right thing to do.

Quin was dressed in his augur's disguise when Lucius arrived. He was explaining to a tavernkeeper that the appearance of seagulls this far inland was most certainly a good omen, and the man would be wise to open his new premises today rather than wait until tomorrow. As soon as he'd taken the man's money and sent him on his way, he turned to Lucius. Quin attempted a cheerful smile, but his eyes were red-rimmed and creased with sadness.

'It's not too late to back out, little brother,' he said after he'd ushered Lucius into his shack and closed the door. 'I can do this.'

Lucius shook his head. 'I've already signed up with Crassus at the ludus. It'll be me in that arena today, and me in the imperial box, killing Glabrio.'

'You're a brave kid,' said Quin. 'Braver than I ever gave you credit for when we were young.'

It felt good to hear the respect in Quin's voice. He so rarely paid Lucius compliments. 'Yours is the harder task, Quin,' he replied. 'Once I've dealt with Glabrio, you've got to get Mother and Val out of his house and take them to a place of safety. It'll be dangerous for a while. His clients and supporters will be out on the streets wanting their own revenge. But eventually, you've got to take back our house and work to restore Father's name.'

'I know what I have to do,' said Quin. 'I just wish I could do all of it and kill Glabrio, too.' He took a bite out of the bread Lucius had brought, then brushed his fingers free of crumbs so he could work on Lucius's make-up. After wiping his face clean, he added fresh smears of swan fat, antimony, ash and kohl. When he'd finished on the face, and straightened the wig to his satisfaction, he showed Lucius a brand-new pair of sandals. 'These were made by a shoemaker I know – cost me a week's auguring wages.' He lifted a flap of leather in the upper sole of the right one to reveal a long, thin compartment containing a small, very sharp dagger no bigger than a stylus.*

Lucius levered it out with his fingernails. His fist completely enclosed the hilt so that only the blade protruded. He practised a few quick stabbing motions. The weapon felt light but comfortable in his hands. He flicked his wrist and the knife tumbled through the air, skewering the remains of the loaf, which Quin had placed on a little side table more than ten feet away.

'Impressive,' observed Quin.

---

* *stylus: a pointed tool for writing on a wax tablet. It is about the same size as a pencil.*

'There were rats on the ship to Ephesus,' explained Lucius. 'We got quite good at impaling them from a distance.'

Quin smiled and nodded. 'By the looks of it, you may not even need to get close to Glabrio.'

Lucius slid the knife back into its compartment and put the sandals on. He winced. 'Not as comfortable as my old pair.'

'Hey, at least they're your size! You weren't there for the fitting.'

'I'm grateful to you,' said Lucius, with a bittersweet smile. He was conscious that time was moving on. 'I'd better get going,' he said, his voice shaking. 'Crassus will be spitting blood if I don't get to the ludus soon.'

Quin hugged him fiercely. Lucius felt the coarse hairs of his brother's false beard against his cheek and smelled his unwashed odour. It reminded him forcefully of the desperate state they were in. If he could only kill Glabrio today, he felt sure that Quin could restore honour and status to the family. His brother's strength bled into him, relaxing the knot in his stomach and planting courage there.

'Together forever!' said Quin.

'Together forever!' Lucius repeated, and this time there was no tremor in his voice.

A shock awaited Lucius when he reached the Ludus Romanus.

'The procurators in charge of the games have handed out this afternoon's pairings,' Crassus informed him when he reported to the lanista's office for duty. 'I'm sorry to inform you that you've been drawn to fight your friend Eprius.'

Lucius's mouth dropped open. 'Can't anything be done, sir?' he pleaded.

'I'm afraid not. You're both unknowns and you've been chosen as a warm-up act to go on straight after lunch before the more famous names make their appearance for the climax of the show.' Crassus looked irritated when Lucius didn't react. 'Look, I don't make the rules, son. Now get out there and start practising. You're on in five hours.'

Lucius found Eprius in the main quadrangle, training on the palus. He cut, thrust and sliced at the wooden pole, making it rotate, then leapt back before getting hit by a sandbag suspended from one of the spinning arms. He stopped when he saw Lucius and came up to him, wiping the sweat from his brow. From his sombre look, Lucius guessed he'd also been told the news.

'Don't fret, old chap,' Eprius said immediately. 'I'll let you win, so you can go up to the box and kill Glabrio.'

'I can't let you do that,' said Lucius miserably. 'They might decide to let you die.'

Eprius shook his head. 'Not if we make it close,' he grinned. 'If I put up a good enough fight, they'll let me live, I'm absolutely certain of it! How about I dominate the first part of the fight – maybe even give you a nick on the arm to make it look real – then you can turn the tables on me. We can rehearse it in the training arena, if you like.'

Lucius sighed. 'I keep thinking of Trebellius, this friend of Quin's that he was forced to kill in the arena. I never want to be in that situation.'

'You won't be,' vowed Eprius. 'Not if we get this right. But whatever happens, I already forgive you, do you understand?'

'I understand,' smiled Lucius.

'Right, let's go and rehearse this fight.'

The shadow on the sundial edged ever closer to noon. Lucius imagined the crowds in the amphitheatre across the way, enjoying the climax of the animal hunts that formed the morning's entertainment. They would be looking forward to lunch and perhaps a few prisoner executions, while their skin was pleasantly cooled by the scented spray jetting from hidden pipes in the walls. Meanwhile, Lucius sweated out the last few hours of his life here in the training arena. Eprius was doing his best to keep him calm and focused as they plotted out the stages of their bout.

'When I make a double feint like this,' Eprius said, demonstrating, 'that'll be the signal for you to drop your guard, exposing yourself to a thrust, and I'll catch you on the arm, like this.'

Lucius tried to concentrate, but he felt as though he was racing towards the edge of a cliff with nothing but darkness beyond. He wished he could slow down the clock. He wanted to see Isi again, one last time, to try and make things better between them. He wished he could have a final conversation with Val, just to tell her how much he loved her and was proud of her. But there was no chance of any of that. The end was closing in fast – much too fast.

He was fighting without real feeling, just going through the motions – reacting, but not coming up with any ideas of his own. Suddenly, Eprius broke off. 'It's not working, old boy. If we fight like this, they'll know something's up. You need to try and surprise me. Do something unexpected and we'll see where it takes us.'

'I'll try,' said Lucius, gritting his teeth and pulling himself together. He made a strike towards Eprius's stomach. Eprius parried, and this time – to vary it – Lucius rotated his blade around the parrying sword to drive a thrust home towards his opponent's chest. Eprius tried to dodge by twisting his torso sideways, but the tip of Lucius's wooden sword caught in his tunic and ripped it.

'That's great!' laughed Eprius, quickly covering his

chest. 'That can be your move – the one that turns the tables on me this afternoon.'

Lucius didn't respond. He'd seen something in the split second that Eprius's chest was exposed, and it chilled him.

'Are you all right, old friend?' Eprius asked him, still pinching closed the ripped tunic with his fingers. 'Tell you what, why don't you give me a moment while I get changed. Then we'll carry on where we left off. That was a truly inspirational move, I must say.'

Lucius's mind was churning as he watched Eprius leave the training arena. There was no doubt about what he'd just seen emblazoned on Eprius's chest: a tattoo of a kestrel, its wings outstretched and tail fanned beneath, with an arrow piercing its heart.

A memory flashed into his mind's eye: Eprius standing there on the deck of the *Cygnus*, looking out to sea, as they arrived back at the ship. He'd looked tanned, yet – now Lucius thought about it – not exactly healthy: his skin had had a sickly greyish tinge, as if he'd been stuck for days in a cabin below decks. Had he followed them from Ephesus, as Isi had suspected? Could he really have been the hooded assassin who killed Canio and released the lion in the arena?

He'd worn a tunic that day, as he always did, even on the hottest days on board the ship, when Lucius, along with the entire crew, had gone bare-chested. He must have done so to hide the tattoo.

But Eprius was his friend! He'd helped him uncover

the truth about Ravilla and Valens. And Lucius had rescued him from cremation in a Pompeii cellar. How could he wear the sign of the kestrel – the sign of Ravilla, whom he knew to be Lucius's enemy?

His father's murderer had the same tattoo on his chest. Could Eprius...

Lucius's mind recoiled from such a thought.

Could Eprius have killed Father?

Impossible! He was a friend – a good and true friend!

Yet how well did Lucius really know him? Their friendship was based on an aquaintance of little more than a week. When he first met him, Eprius had been under the thumb of Valens. It hadn't occurred to him to rebel until Lucius came along and showed him that he could. Maybe Eprius was, at heart, a weak character who expected to be controlled by others. Maybe Glabrio was just the new Valens – the new puppet master pulling Eprius's strings.

It didn't matter. If Eprius turned out to be his father's killer, then Eprius must face the consequences. Lucius felt the onset of a swelling, bursting fury. Blood pounded in his temples. He clenched his fists, trying to calm himself. Before he acted, he would have to question Eprius – give him a chance to explain the tattoo – though he couldn't imagine what possible explanation there could be that didn't point to his guilt.

The wind swirled around the training arena, carrying with it smells of fried food from the square outside, where the crowds had gathered to eat their lunch. Soon it would be time to make his way over to the amphitheatre. Where was Eprius? He should have been back by now. Did he know that Lucius had seen the tattoo? If so, then he was probably busy making his own plans to kill him. Did Eprius plan to kill him in the arena? Glabrio, as sponsor of the games, could easily have arranged the pairing…

Lucius tried to decide what to do. Should he go and hide? But where? Anywhere was better than staying in this small arena, surrounded by high banks of seating, where he could be ambushed from any side.

He left and made his way across the quad, past the ranks of sweating gladiators going through their routines. After mounting some steps, he ran along the shady portico that surrounded the quad, and entered a doorway. He immediately stopped and threw himself behind a pillar, heart thumping wildly. He'd just seen Eprius, now in a different tunic, emerging from one of the dormitories. Lucius risked another peek. Instead of heading back to the quad, Eprius had turned left and was making for the southern end of the ludus. Where was he going? There was nothing there but slave quarters and storerooms. Lucius decided to follow, darting from pillar to pillar and keeping as quiet as possible.

At the southwestern corner of the building, Eprius passed beneath an archway and descended some steps. Lucius was momentarily confused – he didn't remember there being a stairway here during his days working at the ludus. The wedge-shaped stones above the archway looked freshly hewn, and the steps leading downwards appeared new. Where could this lead? Once Eprius's figure had disappeared into the shadows, Lucius began making his own way down the steps. At the bottom lay a narrow, straight tunnel, lit at regular intervals by burning torches in brackets. Every sound echoed down here, and Lucius had to be especially quiet as he crept forward.

Soon enough, familiar smells and sounds began to reach him – musky animal odours, grunts and growls – and he was instantly taken back to his days working in the basement, or hypogeum, beneath the amphitheatre. Of course! That was where the tunnel was leading! It must have been built for the safety of the gladiators, so they could access the amphitheatre without having to traverse the square above, with its screaming fans. The tunnel eventually opened out into the cavernous setting of the hypogeum. He glimpsed filthy, straw-filled cages where sluggish-looking animals lay, idly flicking their tails. He looked around for Eprius, and soon spotted his tall, slim figure standing in the shadow of an elevator shaft. Lucius slipped out of sight behind a thick travertine pillar.

Eprius was not alone. He was with an older man, dressed in the purple-edged toga of a senior magistrate. Torchlight glistened waxily on the man's narrow, skull-like face, with its high cheekbones, hooded eyes and hooked nose. He murmured something into Eprius's ear, then passed him a small glass bottle drawn from within the folds of his toga. Lucius recognised the man immediately. He'd seen him in the Forum and at the Circus Maximus. He was Consul Marcus Acilius Glabrio, and the fact that Eprius was talking with him was proof, if any were still needed, that Eprius was the hooded assassin.

Lucius felt the rage welling up within him again, and he was shocked by its ferocity. His hatred of Eprius was like a fire inside him, made all the more intense by a devastating sense of betrayal. He wished now that he'd left him to die in Pompeii. He tried to channel his anger in the way that he'd learnt from Hierax. Forcing his breathing under control, he tried to think in cold, logical steps. If he was quick, and accurate, he could deal with both of them right now. Very quietly, he reached down and removed his right sandal, then felt for the little compartment containing the knife.

But before the knife was fully in his hand and the sandal back on his foot, Glabrio had moved away, melting into the shadows. Lucius emerged from the pillar and started after the consul, but stopped as Eprius shifted into his path.

Lucius snarled, showing his teeth. 'Get out of my way, you swine.' The blade glittered in Lucius's hand. He was pleased to see the nervousness on Eprius's face as he glanced down at the knife.

Eprius tried to cover it up with a snort of laughter.

'I say, old boy, isn't it bad luck for us to meet so soon before the fight?'

'I should kill you now,' breathed Lucius, taking aim at Eprius's heart. 'I've skewered much smaller rats from this range.'

He was about to let fly when his wrist was grabbed by a powerful hand. The hand squeezed and went on squeezing until Lucius felt like howling, and the knife dropped with a clatter to the floor. The assailant bent Lucius's arm behind his back and shoved him painfully to his knees. The whines of the animals echoed around him as they sensed the violent disturbance, but Crassus's voice cut through the cacophany. 'I thought this kid was supposed to be your friend!' he bellowed, close to Lucius's ear. The lanista looked up at Eprius. 'You all right?'

'Fine, thank you!' replied Eprius, looking much more cheerful.

'I came to tell you that you're due on in five minutes, so get upstairs to the waiting area, get your armour on and await your call.

'Of course,' said Eprius, dashing off.

Lucius retrieved the dropped knife and was about to follow Eprius when Crassus grabbed him by the scruff of his tunic and pulled him up close. 'Hand it over,' he scowled. Lucius sighed and placed the knife in his palm. 'I don't care what the history is between you two,' Crassus muttered darkly, 'but that boy belongs to me now, and if I ever see you try to kill him again – outside the arena, that is – I'll put you in a cell on your own and you won't see daylight for six weeks. Are we clear?'

Lucius nodded sullenly. He'd been seconds away from killing his father's murderer. Now his act of vengeance would have to be carried out in public, in front of sixty thousand spectators...

CHAPTER XIV

19 APRIL

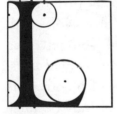ucius climbed some steps to the corridor that led to the entry gate to the arena. An attendant, waiting for him at the top, showed him into a small room adjoining the corridor, where his armour and weapons were waiting for him. There was no sign of Eprius.

'We have found that it's better to keep opponents apart before the bout,' the attendant replied to his unspoken question.

As the attendant began strapping on his manica, leg padding and greaves, Lucius tried to focus on the contest to come, but all he could think about was his own stupidity. Why hadn't he listened to Isi's advice and said goodbye to Eprius as soon as they got to

Rome? By confiding in him, he had wrecked any chance he might have had of killing Glabrio. Eprius would have told the consul everything – and now there was no way he was going to be invited into the imperial box after the fight – not that it mattered, now he'd lost the knife. Revenge on Glabrio would have to wait for another day. This afternoon, though, he could at least inflict blood vengeance in the arena by killing Glabrio's 'weapon', Eprius – the murderer of Lucius's father.

The attendant handed him his sword, and he ran his finger slowly along the length of its gleaming blade, imagining Eprius's blood dripping from it. For a brief moment he was reminded of Isi's words to him last night, when she had questioned his 'obsession' with avenging his father. 'You Romans think yourselves so civilised,' she'd said in that self-righteous way of hers, 'but your whole history is just a series of bloody acts of revenge. You slaughtered the tribes of Italy because they dared to stand up to you, then turned your vengeful rage on the Carthaginians, and the thousands of slaves crucified on the Via Appia, and the peoples of Gaul and Britannia, and the Jews of Jerusalem – all because they had the nerve to try and fight back against your all-conquering legions. But it's not the only way. You can be better than that, Lucius…'

He had dismissed her words then, but now he wondered whether this murderous anger inside him really was a good thing. Was it really what his father would have wanted? He wished he knew the answer to that question.

A slave came in bearing a cup of posca. This was the traditional drink of vinegar, water, honey and flavouring herbs, served to gladiators before a bout. Lucius had never much liked the taste, but he gulped some of it down anyway. It was even more bitter than the brews he'd been offered in Carthage and Ephesus, and half of it remained in the cup when he handed it back.

'Time to go,' said the attendant. Strapping on his shield and picking up his spear and helmet, Lucius followed the attendant out of the room and down the corridor to the gate. Dusty sunlight poured through the bars. There was a smell of freshly spilt blood, and the chanting of the crowd had the urgency of animals clamouring to be fed.

Eprius was already there at the gate, looking tall and impressive in his Murmillo outfit, his helmet cradled on his forearm. He turned as Lucius approached, and smiled, his face as open and innocent as ever. 'I killed your father,' he said pleasantly, 'and now I shall kill you.'

His chest was bare, and Lucius could see the kestrel tattoo in all its ugly glory. He wanted to cut the boy's throat there and then, but resisted the urge. If Eprius desired a fight to the death, Lucius would give him one. Besides, before he killed him, he needed some sort of explanation.

'Why, Eprius?' he murmured. 'After Pompeii!'

The smile twisted into a sneer, and for the first time Lucius glimpsed the true nature of his former friend. 'You rescued me from Vesuvius, but for what? To leave me like a stray dog on the streets of Rome? You never cared for me, Lucius. I opened your eyes to the truth about Valens, but you never thanked me. I had no family, no friends to turn to once we got to Rome, and you knew that.'

A horn blared and the gate opened.

'Out you go,' grunted a guard, and suddenly they were walking side by side across the blazing white sand, half-deafened by the roar of the crowd and the strains of the hydraulic organ.* As they made their way towards the centre of the arena where the summa rudis and his attendants stood waiting, they waved dutifully at the crowd, and Eprius turned and shouted into Lucius's ear: 'I nearly died of starvation, thanks to you. Eventually, I threw myself at the mercy of Glabrio, an old acquaintance of my father's. He took me in and fed me. He showered me with every kindness…'

He broke off and glanced towards the imperial box, where the consul sat watching intently. Did some secret communication pass between them then? It might have been Lucius's imagination, but they seemed to exchange a look. He wondered if they had some plan

---

* *hydraulic organ: an organ worked by water pressure, which made a powerful sound but could be played with a light touch.*

for the fight – some means of guaranteeing victory for Eprius. That bottle that Glabrio had handed to Eprius in the hypogeum – could it have been poison? He remembered Eprius telling him once that gladiators had been known to dip their swords in poison before a fight, so that one nick from their blade would be fatal. He glanced at Eprius's sword, swinging from his belt. There was no obvious discolouration on the tip, but he'd learned not to judge anything by appearances – the poison could be colourless.

They reached the centre, and another blast from the horns was the signal for the crowd to fall quiet. As an official introduced the bout, Eprius leaned close and cupped his hand to Lucius's ear so he could hear every word: 'Glabrio taught me the truth about your family. He told me how together you destroyed the noble Ravilla. He trained me in combat, espionage and assassination. Then he sent me out to kill your father, and I did it – gladly! After that, he sent me to Ephesus to deal with that other enemy of the state, Canio.' He chuckled. 'And I was most grateful to you for leading me to him.'

Lucius trembled to think of the lies Glabrio must have fed Eprius. The noble Ravilla indeed! And Canio, an enemy of the state? – when his only crime had been to witness Glabrio's poisoning of Titus.

There was so much he wanted to say to Eprius – to try and make him understand how he'd been tricked and manipulated – but there was no time, and he wasn't sure he'd be able to express himself properly anyway. It may have been the heat and the tension, but he was starting to feel quite dizzy.

Before Lucius felt fully ready, the summa rudis called for the fight to begin. He jammed on his helmet and felt the usual terrifying sensation of claustrophobia as his world shrank to two tiny portholes of sunlight and sand. He swung around trying to catch sight of Eprius, and found that his opponent had already crept behind him and was closing in fast. Lucius had to scramble to stay out of range. As they circled each other, Eprius goaded him with darting flashes of his sword. Lucius tried to focus on the tip – he knew he had to avoid the slightest cut – but the blade kept dancing this way and that, teasing him like the head of a cobra, and it only increased his dizziness. Remembering his technique, he kept his sword low and away from his body, his spear hoisted above his shoulder, parallel to the ground. His body knew what to do – if only his head would clear.

Eprius took an audible breath and came at him suddenly with a shield barge. Lucius had heard the breath and tried to dodge, but his legs were sluggish for some reason and he found himself falling heavily on his side. He rolled away just as Eprius's sword sliced downward, missing him by inches. He clambered back to his feet just in time to parry a series of rapid vertical cuts aimed at his head. They locked swords, and he managed to shove Eprius away, making him stagger backward. This should have encouraged Lucius, but he knew things still weren't right. His footwork was lethargic, his strokes flailing and inaccurate, and his head felt as though it was stuffed with feathers.

He caught sight of Eprius's face smirking behind the grille of his visor. 'Enjoy your posca, then?' he laughed.

And that was when Lucius knew what had happened: the bottle Glabrio had given him must have contained some sort of drug, which Eprius then managed to slip into Lucius's posca. Thank Fortuna he hadn't drunk it all!

Lucius blazed with anger. The cheats! The cowards! Not even prepared to engage him in an honest fight, they'd hobbled him from the start to ensure he'd never have a chance. This was murder in the guise of fair combat!

With a roar of frustration, Lucius hurled his spear straight at Eprius's head. Eprius casually batted it aside with his shield, and cackled once more. Now Lucius had nothing to fight with but a small circular shield and his gladius – and his vision had begun to swim. He swung his sword at Eprius and then staggered, off balance. Ahead of him loomed another Eprius carrying a double-headed hammer. He swung at him once more, which provoked a chorus of jeers from the crowd. He blinked, and his vision cleared enough for him to see he'd nearly decapitated an official dressed as Charun, the demon whose job was to carry the deceased through the Gate of the Dead. He heard scattered laughter around the stadium. Maybe they thought he was drunk!

Before he could find the real Eprius, a searing pain struck his arm. Eprius had attacked from behind. Lucius saw his own blood dripping onto the sand and knew that only the manica had prevented an amputation. Drenched in sweat, he turned to face his enemy. Eprius bobbed and weaved in front of him, darting forward to execute a vicious downward swinging cut to Lucius's left leg. But Lucius had heard the breath preceding the attack and this time managed to parry and execute a little counterthrust of his own – the pain seemed to have woken him up a little.

It wasn't enough, though – the fog in his head was costing him vital seconds in the battle of speed and thought. This was a fight he could and should have won – that was the infuriating thing! Whatever happened, he vowed he would go down fighting. Brushing his opponent's sword aside, he launched himself at him with a rapid sequence of cuts and thrusts. It felt good, but it wasn't like the smooth, devastating assault he'd inflicted on Hierax or the Murmillo in Ephesus. Hatred alone, however intense, couldn't compensate for a weakened body. His strikes lacked accuracy, speed and penetration, and were easily blocked.

He knew it was only a matter of time before he faltered. The effort of attacking with his sword and maintaining his guard was becoming too much. The crowd, he vaguely sensed, were cheering him on. They liked the fact that he was pushing Eprius steadily back, but they had no idea that he was fighting at his very limits – maybe even beyond them. Sooner than expected, his defences slipped and Eprius struck with a hard punch of his shield boss into Lucius's stomach. The wind flew out of his lungs and hope fled from his heart as he crashed backward onto the sand. He lay there, chest heaving, listening to his own wheezing attempts to gather in more air. His eyes flickered open to see Eprius grinning down at him from above the gleaming slope of his sword, its tip pressed to Lucius's exposed throat.

'Like father, like son,' sniggered Eprius. 'Dying on your back.'

The summa rudis stood close by, waiting for Lucius to signal his surrender. Whatever the crowd pleaded, Lucius already knew Glabrio's decision. Surrender could only mean death.

Gradually, his breath returned and his mind grew calmer. He wasn't scared of death, just hated the idea that it was coming now, before he'd managed to do his duty. There had to be another way...

'Raise your finger if you want to stop the fight,' the summa rudis prompted.

Lucius didn't move.

Eprius stood tall and proud above him, and Lucius noted the position of his enemy's feet, very close to his own right ankle.

'Surrender, Lucius,' Eprius purred.

'Never,' screamed Lucius, and he lifted both feet and rammed them hard into Eprius's shins.

Eprius screamed in pain. He frantically wheeled his arms, trying to stay upright, but fell hard on his back.

A divine energy seemed to possess Lucius at that moment – where it came from he had no idea – but he rose, quicker than smoke, and before Eprius even opened his eyes, the tables had been turned. When Eprius looked up it was to see Lucius's sword tip pressed to his own throat.

'Punic Surprise, old boy,' murmured Lucius, and he couldn't resist a smile.

'What?' spluttered Eprius.

'Just a little trick I learned in Carthage.'

Eprius banged his fist against the ground in frustration, raising a cloud of dust.

'So, what's it to be, then?' Lucius asked him. 'Surrender?'

Eprius managed a sour smile as he raised his finger, signalling to the summa rudis to end the contest. 'This round to you,' he murmured. 'But I'll survive today – Glabrio will see to that. And then I'll come back and kill you.'

Eprius didn't seem to have won many admirers among the spectators, because a clear majority were howling 'Iugula! Iugula!' Yet he appeared serene and confident as he and Lucius looked up towards the imperial box and awaited the verdict.

The consul's face was a mask, giving no sign of his feelings one way or the other. Yet his hesitation was clearly irritating the crowd, many of whom had begun to jeer. Finally, he stood, and the crowd roared its excitement, their chants for death growing ever wilder. Glabrio raised his arm and revealed his hand with the thumb jabbing out like a knife blade to one side – the sign for death.

'No!' shrieked Eprius. 'No!'

There was a hunger and anticipation in the wall of noise surrounding them – like the baying of wolves. Lucius moved the sword downwards from Eprius's throat until it reached the tattoo on his chest. He positioned the tip of the blade against the kestrel's heart, exactly where it was pierced by the arrow. Eprius's chest rose and fell in violent gasps as he stared wildly at Lucius, giving the illusion that his tattoo had come to life. For a brief moment, the kestrel almost appeared to fly – until Lucius's sword thrust downwards and the bird became still.

Cheers erupted in the stands. 'Alecto! Alecto! Alecto!' they cried. Lucius acknowledged the tribute by raising his sword. Eprius was dead, yet he felt no euphoria, only a grim sort of satisfaction. All the pain and exhaustion he'd blocked out during the fight now threatened to overwhelm him, and it was a struggle just to remain on his feet. His legs felt numb and shaky, his wounded arm was one long shout of pain, and his head throbbed as though it was being pounded with stones. He longed to be able to lie down somewhere and rest, but he knew he remained in deadly danger. He could see Glabrio, up in the imperial box, leaning back in his chair and whispering something in the ear of a Praetorian guard. The guard immediately departed through an exit to the rear. Lucius realised that as soon as he left the arena and was out of the public gaze, Glabrio's soldiers would close in on him and finish off what Eprius had failed to do.

Slaves led by Charun, the demon, were carrying Eprius's body towards the Gate of Death, while others were busy raking over the bloody patches on the sand. An official approached Lucius. 'You've warmed them up nicely,' he chuckled, 'but we'd be obliged if you'd clear off now, so we can bring on our star attractions.' He began bustling Lucius back towards the Gate of Life – the gate through which he'd entered – on the eastern side of the arena.

At the gate, Lucius was handed over to an attendant whose job was to divest him of his armour and weapons. After that, he would be escorted down a stairway and along the underground passageway that led back to the ludus. He doubted he would ever resurface from that tunnel. Glabrio's men would probably kill him down there, out of sight of any witnesses – Crassus would be compensated for the loss of a gladiator, and if anyone ever asked what had happened to 'Alecto', they'd be told he'd met with an accident.

Lucius knew that if he had any chance of surviving the next few minutes, he would have to act now. He drew his sword and swung its flat side hard at the attendant's head. 'Sorry,' he whispered as the man slumped, senseless, to the floor. Then he ran, as fast as his sluggish limbs would allow, towards the amphitheatre's east entrance at the far end of the corridor. Two guards had been posted there for the very purpose of preventing gladiators from escaping. As Lucius ran towards them they shifted into a defensive posture, raising their spears threateningly. Through the arched entrance behind them, Lucius glimpsed sunlight on the square and carefree citizens wandering past the ornamental fountain, the Meta Sudans. He could throw off his armour and lose himself in those crowds – freedom was just yards away. But the guards were big, solid-looking men, and they had no intention of letting him through.

Lucius slowed to a halt, desperately casting around for another possible exit. The walls to either side of him were lined with archways, but unfortunately every one of them was bricked up.

'Maybe you're lost,' one of the guards said with mock courtesy. 'The stairs back to the tunnel are right behind you if you'd care to take them.'

Just then, there was a commotion on the square: sounds of marching and cries of citizens being pushed aside, as ranks of white-crested Praetorian guards came into view. Lucius felt his hopes sinking at the sight. Yet the Praetorians were still a good distance away – there could yet be time to break out of here. He hoped the two guards would be distracted by the noise and perhaps turn to see what was going on, but neither took their eyes off him for a second.

His only hope, he realised, was to head back to the ludus and try to escape from there. He turned and started back up the corridor towards the stairway that led to the tunnel. Maybe there wouldn't be any soldiers down there waiting to ambush him. But even as he thought this, he heard the sounds of iron-shod sandals echoing on stone, and he saw the white-plumed helmets of Praetorians mounting the stairway towards him. They were closing in on all sides. In despair he raced back towards the guards at the east entrance. He would fight, and go on fighting, till he drew his last breath.

But as he approached the guards, an extraordinary thing happened. A pair of figures suddenly appeared behind them and struck them hard over the head with wooden sticks. The guards tumbled, dazed, to the floor. Lucius nearly fell over himself with amazement and delight as he saw who had carried out this surprise attack.

'Quick,' yelled Isi, grabbing his arm. As the Praetorians jogged towards them, swords raised, she pushed him beneath the canvas of a covered wagon that had pulled up just outside the entrance. It looked like one of the supply vehicles that ferried scenery and machinery for battle re-enactments from the storehouse known as the Summum Choragium to the amphitheatre. Quin, in his augur outfit, was the other member of the rescue team, and was already back in the driver's seat of the wagon. As soon as Isi and Lucius were aboard, he cracked the whip and began racing through the square. Lucius peered out from beneath the canvas to see pigeons and pedestrians scattering before them as they clattered along the cobbles.

For a while, as they sped through the city, Lucius could only gasp and stare, unable to speak – just revelling in the fact that he was still alive.

'How?' he finally managed to splutter to Isi. 'How did you know where I'd be?'

He could barely see her in the shadows beneath the canvas, and could only just make out her shouted explanation above the rattle of cartwheels: 'Durio, my old friend at the ludus, told me that Eprius had been spotted with the tattoo – a slave had seen it while he was changing. That's when I knew I'd been right about him. He also said you two had been drawn to fight each other. We figured out the plan then, your brother and I. We knew Eprius was supposed to kill you in the arena, and we reckoned that if you survived, you'd need a quick getaway. When we heard them chanting 'Alecto', we knew you'd won and we guessed you'd be clever and try to escape through the east entrance, so this is where we came. Quin got hold of the wagon. The horses aren't the regular sort, though.

They're special – borrowed from his friend Pertinax at the Circus Maximus.'

Lucius laughed when he heard this. He took another peep out of the back of the wagon. They were speeding along the Via Labicana, heading east out of the city. There was no sign of any pursuing Praetorians – their mode of escape must have taken Glabrio and everyone else completely by surprise.

'I'm sorry I didn't believe you about Eprius,' Lucius told her.

She reached forward then and hugged him, and her tears wet his cheeks.

'I'm proud of you,' she said.

END OF BOOK 4

AUTHOR'S NOTE

The death of the emperor Titus is a historical mystery. The Greek writer Flavius Philostratus claims he was poisoned by his brother Domitian with a sea-hare and that his death was foretold by Apollonius of Tyana (who would also go on to foretell Domitian's death). Roman historian Aurelius Victor also states that Titus was poisoned. However, Suetonius and Cassius Dio record that he died of natural causes. For the purposes of my plot, I have gone with the murder scenario. Titus's final words, 'I have made but one mistake,' have been the source of much speculation by historians then and since. I have given them my own interpretation.

In the Ephesus section of my story, the fictional character Canio is living with a Christian named John. He is based on St John the Apostle, author of the Gospel of John. According to tradition, John lived to a ripe old age and spent much of his later life in Ephesus.

FOLLOW LUCIUS'S FURTHER ADVENTURES IN:

GLADIATOR SCHOOL 5
BLOOD AND THUNDER

ucius, Quintus and Isidora descended the Palatine Hill by the Steps of Cacus. This ornamental stairway, decorated with terraced flowerbeds, wound down the side of the hill towards the crowded cattle market, the Forum Boarium, and beyond that to the river. After passing through the market, they walked along the riverfront, heading north towards their hideout near the vegetable market, the Forum Holitorium.

'What are all those people doing down there by the riverbank?' asked Isi suddenly. The other two turned to see where she was pointing. They had just passed the multi-arched bridge known as the Pons Aemilius, where the Tiber bent westwards along the southern border of the Campus Martius. On the muddy banks near the first of the bridge's arches, a small group of people had gathered. A couple of them were dragging something out of the water. Lucius, Quin and Isi drew closer, and let out a collective gasp when they saw what it was: the body of a man.

The dead man's flesh was mottled and bluish after its long submersion in water. There were signs of bruising on his skin. His grey hair and the bald spot on his crown gave Lucius the impression of a meek and gentle man, undeserving of this horrid fate.

'He's probably just an old slave from Tiber Island who'd had enough,' said Quin. Tiber Island was an islet in the middle of the river just a short way upstream. It was inhabited by elderly or sick slaves who had been abandoned by their masters.

'But look at his toga,' said Isi. 'He must have been wealthy.'

The boys looked, and had to agree with her. The toga, though sodden and caked in the filth of the river, appeared to be of good-quality material.

A cry went up from one of the women gathered near the body: 'Gods! It's Diomedes!'

The news passed swiftly among the others on the riverbank, and Lucius heard the name repeated like an echo: 'It's Diomedes!... Diomedes!... Diomedes!' Even those who had congregated on the bridge above, and on the waterfront, took up the cry. 'Diomedes... Diomedes is dead!'

'Who is Diomedes?' one young man nervously asked.

'You don't know who Diomedes is?' another replied accusingly, before turning to his friend and declaring incredulously: 'He doesn't know who Diomedes is!'

From the general confused muttering, Lucius concluded that not many people actually knew who Diomedes was, only that he was someone important. Lucius himself thought he'd heard the name mentioned once or twice, possibly by his father, but he, too, couldn't remember who the man was. Eventually, the woman who'd originally identified him put everyone out of their misery. 'Diomedes,' she said, 'was personal physician to our beloved former emperor and now god, Titus.'

Everyone then turned with renewed interest to the corpse lying on the mud, getting splashed by the murky brown waters of the river. It seemed almost impossible to believe that those blotchy, swollen hands had once tended to the medical needs of the most powerful man on earth.

TO BE CONTINUED...

A selected list of Scribo titles

The prices shown below are correct at the time of going to press. However, The Salariya Book Company reserves the right to show new retail prices on covers, which may differ from those previously advertised.

Gladiator School by Dan Scott

1	Blood Oath	978-1-908177-48-3	£6.99
2	Blood & Fire	978-1-908973-60-3	£6.99
3	Blood & Sand	978-1-909645-16-5	£6.99
4	Blood Vengeance	978-1-909645-62-2	£6.99
5	Blood & Thunder *(Autumn 2014)*		
		978-1-910184-20-2	£6.99

Aldo Moon by Alex Woolf

1 Aldo Moon and the Ghost at Gravewood Hall		
	978-1-908177-84-1	£6.99

Chronosphere by Alex Woolf

1	Time out of Time	978-1-907184-55-0	£6.99
2	Malfunction	978-1-907184-56-7	£6.99
3	Ex Tempora	978-1-908177-87-2	£6.99

Visit our website at:

www.salariya.com

All Scribo and Salariya Book Company titles can be ordered from your local bookshop, or by post from:

The Salariya Book Co. Ltd,
25 Marlborough Place
Brighton BN1 1UB

Postage and packing **free** in the United Kingdom